Turning HEARTS

a novel

Deanne Blackhurst

Covenant Communications, Inc.

Cover image: *Female Portrait* © Lucas Cornwell; courtesy of iStock Photo

Cover design © 2010 by Covenant Communications, Inc.

Published by Covenant Communications, Inc.
American Fork, Utah

Printed in Canada
First Printing: April 2010

16 15 14 13 12 11 10   10 9 8 7 6 5 4 3 2 1

ISBN-13: 978-1-59811-541-3
ISBN-10: 1-59811-541-3

To all the elders and sisters who have served, are serving, or will serve
in the great army of God, spreading the gospel throughout the world.
But especially to those wonderful missionaries whom I have had
the honor of working with personally.

Acknowledgments

THIS WORK HAS BEEN A long time in the making. Through it all I have had the opportunity to learn from many talented wordsmiths. I'd like to thank B. J. Rowley and Valerie Holladay for the countless hours they spent working with me and teaching me the craft. To Kirk Shaw, my editor, and all the people at Covenant Communications who've turned my pile of manuscript pages into a real book, and to Richard, who, for some unknown reason, believed in me from the start.

I'd like to give thanks to my gifted friends from the Refiner's Fire Critique Group, who spent many afternoons and evenings helping me to edit and polish my story, and to the Sycamore/DeKalb book club members, who offered terrific suggestions and much-needed support. And I cannot forget the many returned sister missionaries through the years who have shared their stories and their testimonies with me.

I feel tremendous appreciation to my parents, Richard and Vicki Savage; my sister, Kathy Clement; Don and Jennifer Blackhurst; and the late Barbara Martin, who struggled through countless early manuscripts, searching for inconsistencies and typos. And to my brother and his wife, Jeff and Jennifer Savage, who helped me keep my direction clear and my street language believable.

My children, Ryan and Tiffany, Antonio, Steven, Jeremy, Annese, and Joshua, provided what any author needs most—time to work and cooperation when dinner was late and the laundry went unfolded. Thanks to them for their love and patience. And last—but most important—my husband, Kent, the man who has shared my joys, my sorrows, and my dreams for the past twenty-four years and who makes everything I've ever done possible.

Prologue

THE RECURRING DREAM HAD FIRST begun when Amanda Kelly was a senior in high school. She didn't usually take note of such things; quite often she didn't even remember her dreams by the time she was fully awake. But this dream was different, and it always began the same way.

She stood in the living room of a strange house, staring at a wall covered from top to bottom with pictures. At least a hundred photos were displayed in ornate frames and protected behind clear glass plates. There were black-and-white photos of smiling babies. Family groups dressed in styles of yesteryear stared stoically out at the world. On the top left was an eight-by-ten of a couple on their wedding day and underneath it, the portrait of a young soldier in his dress uniform.

Before her death, Grandma Howard had collected family pictures like this and displayed them on the wall next to the stairs in her home. Amanda could remember slowly ascending the stairs, step by step, studying each face in detail, trying to find features similar to her own. The same gray-green eyes, upturned nose, or long blond hair.

But in this dream, the people in the pictures were all unknown to her. As she began to turn away, a shiny gold frame drew her attention. Something about the faces smiling out at her seemed vaguely familiar. She stepped closer and reached toward it, but before she could touch it the portrait disappeared. One minute it was there, the next it was gone, leaving a gaping hole in the jigsaw puzzle of frames.

A deep sadness overwhelmed Amanda, as if something of great value had been lost. She searched the wall again and again, but it didn't matter. The picture was gone.

Sensing a presence in the room, Amanda turned to find her Grandma Howard watching from the door and smiling tenderly at her granddaughter. "They're lost, and it's up to you to find them," her grandmother said.

Though softly spoken, her words contained a sense of urgency that was almost palpable.

"I don't understand," Amanda cried. "Who are they and what am I supposed to do?"

"The family members are lost and you must find them. You're the only one who can."

The dream would end there, and as she awoke, the sound of her grandmother's voice echoed in her mind. "You must find them. You're the only one who can."

Every detail of the dream remained crystal clear in Amanda's memory except one. No matter how hard she tried, she could never recall the faces from the missing picture.

Chapter One

Text message sent April 8, 2008, at 10:57 AM
Amanda, I thought about it all night. You should do what you think is right.
Will be there at dinner. Love U.

"JAKE AND I HAVE DECIDED to put off the wedding."

It was a Sunday evening, and the family had just finished dinner. Her mother, at the sink doing dishes, froze at her words. Her father, still sitting at the table, stared at her in dismay.

"I mean, it's not like we're never going to get married," she said quickly, turning to Jake who sat beside her. He'd driven down from his home in Idaho Falls to spend the weekend with her. "It's just that it won't happen at the end of the month like we planned."

For a moment the room was silent except for a slight buzzing noise coming from the overhead light fixture.

"But why?" her mother asked at last. "You both seem so happy together."

"Is it a worthiness issue?" Her father turned a grim eye on Jake, who blushed.

"No, sir, of course not. It's nothing like that."

Jake hadn't really understood her reasons. Still, he was here beside her to lend his support.

"Then why?" her mother repeated.

Amanda took a deep breath and tried to stop her hands from clenching the edge of the table. "Because I've decided to go on a mission."

"But I thought you'd already decided that your mission was to get married and raise a righteous family," her father said.

Amanda could hear the accusation in his voice.

Her mother moved to the table and sat down in a chair across from her daughter. "You can't do this. We've sent invitations out; your Aunt Grace in Maryland has already bought her plane ticket for Salt Lake. The ladies in Relief Society are giving you a shower at the end of the week. What am I supposed to tell them?"

Her father had moved from shock to anger. "Do you know how much money we've spent on this wedding already? Your dress, the cake, the deposit on the room at the Lion House, and now you just want to call it off?"

She looked at her parents' faces and felt terrible. It was clear they felt hurt and betrayed. This was even worse than she'd imagined.

Calling off her wedding had been the most difficult thing she'd ever had to do. She did love Jake, but the strong feelings that compelled her to serve could not be ignored.

"Jake is so terrific," her mother said with tears in her eyes. "We all love him, and he loves you."

"This isn't about love. This is something I have to do."

Her mother tried again. "You could serve a mission with Jake when you get older. You don't have to do it now. Or maybe you could serve a ward mission."

Jake looked up hopefully, but Amanda didn't even try to argue. She just shook her head.

"Fine." Her mother stood up and moved behind Jake. She glared at her daughter while resting her hands possessively on Jake's shoulders. "You can do whatever you like, but I'm not going to lose Jake. I'll . . . I'll adopt him if I have to."

"Mom! Dad! I'm sorry. I don't mean to hurt you, but I have to go!" Amanda fought to hold back tears of frustration. "Can't you just trust me on this? It's what I'm supposed to do."

* * *

That night as Amanda stood at her bedroom window staring down at the glittering lights of the Salt Lake Valley below, she went over the scene again and again in her mind. She knew how nebulous her reasons sounded, and she didn't blame her parents for reacting as they had. And yet, how was she supposed to deny the sense of urgency she felt whenever she thought of the family she'd been sent to search for in her dream?

And it wasn't just the dream. There had been other things as well. Small moments when the Spirit had spoken to her heart and added to her certainty.

Like that night in December right after Jake got home from his mission to Canada, when the two of them sat in his car outside her apartment talking for hours.

Jake told her about the people he'd taught and shared some of his unique experiences. Amanda could still remember the snow falling silently, burying the car in a layer of glittering white fluff. Inside, the Spirit felt like a soft, cozy blanket keeping her warm and safe.

Just before he got out to open her door, Jake had put his arm around Amanda and pulled her close. "It's funny, but I think the most amazing thing about my mission wasn't the stuff that happened around me, but the stuff that happened inside me. Does that make any sense?"

He tried to explain. "I've been a member of the Church all my life. I went to Primary, Sunday School, youth conferences, seminary . . . all that. I knew about Jesus and Heavenly Father, and I always thought that was enough. But on my mission, I actually got to know Them, not just know about Them. I gained this incredible personal relationship . . . this one-on-one thing. It's like, I always believed, but now I know!"

She'd envied the confidence and the power she'd sensed from him as he'd said those words, and she felt an irresistible desire to have those same experiences for herself. She would have them.

* * *

July 31, 2008

Dear Amanda,

Wow—I can't believe you've been in the MTC for a whole week. The California San Jose Mission won't know what hit 'em when you get there. BYU starts up in a little less than a month, and I'm hoping that I haven't gotten too rusty after being away for almost three years.

I wish you were going to be here taking classes with me. I miss you so much, but I'm really proud of you too.

I love you forever,
Jake

* * *

"It wasn't that bad. Really," Sister Baker, Amanda's MTC companion, said, sitting down on the bed next to her companion.

Amanda pulled her knees up to her chest and struggled to control the humiliation and embarrassment flooding over her. She wouldn't make it worse by crying like a child. She'd only been in the MTC a few weeks, and already she felt completely out of control.

"The media center can be unpredictable," Sister Baker continued. "Remember last week? That woman called and asked me how any grown adult could believe in all that Joseph Smith fairy-tale stuff. My clever comeback was 'Fairy tales aren't just for children.' Talk about completely stupid."

Amanda smiled weakly. "Sister Baker, no offense, but that was nothing compared to the mess I made today."

"Oh, come on, the fanatical call was priceless."

"Maybe for you."

Each week the missionaries were given the assignment to answer calls in the MTC Media Center. People from all over the country called in after seeing Church ads on television or hearing them on the radio. They could ask questions or order free scriptures or DVDs about the Church.

The first time she'd worked on the phones, Amanda had been a little nervous, but it hadn't turned out to be as bad as she'd expected. It wasn't until halfway through her second shift that she'd received "the call from hell."

"Do you believe that you will someday be a god, and equal in every way to God, our Father?" screeched an irate female voice before Amanda could even say hello.

She felt disconcerted, wondering if she'd pushed the wrong button by mistake and picked up an ongoing call.

"Excuse me?" Amanda stammered.

The woman's voice grew even louder as she spoke. "You cannot be excused for blasphemy. You are going to hell, where you will burn forever!"

A surge of anger rushed through Amanda in response to the aggression in the caller's voice. "Obviously you don't know much about the Mormons."

The woman was screaming now. "They brainwash people, those Mormons do. Get away before it's too late!"

"You don't even know what we believe," Amanda snapped sharply, raising her voice to be heard over the woman's ranting on the other end. "How can you presume to judge us?"

The other missionaries in the room had stopped what they were doing and turned around to stare at her.

"An everlasting hell where you will burn forever but never be consumed—"

Click.

The screaming in her ear abruptly changed to silence as Amanda hung up on the caller.

Her hands shaking, she accidentally knocked the keyboard off the desk, and Brother Daniels, the media center director, picked it up.

"Get back to your calls," he instructed the other missionaries before turning to Amanda. He pushed his glasses a little higher on his nose and spoke in a comforting voice. "It's okay, don't take it personally, Sister. Some people are like that. They don't care who they're talking to. They just want to vent."

"But how can I not take it personally? I didn't know what to say or what to do; I totally froze up."

"You're being too hard on yourself. Lighten up a little." He smiled. "It wasn't that long ago that I was serving a full-time mission, and one thing I learned was that you can either laugh your way through rejection or cry your way through. I'd recommend the former."

It was good advice, but Amanda wasn't sure she could follow it.

* * *

August 1, 2008

Dearest Jake,

By this time next week I will be on the streets of San Jose finding the Savior's lost sheep and teaching them the gospel. I'm excited but a little scared too. The MTC has been great, but I'm anxious to get out in the field. At the same time, I'm just not sure if I'm as prepared as I want to be. Did you feel this way when you first arrived in Quebec?

Have I told you lately what a fabulous boyfriend you are and how much I appreciate all your love and support? I couldn't do this without you. I love you so much, and I can't wait until we are sealed together forever.

Love you always,
Amanda

A feeling of excitement filled the air as the sister missionaries drifted into the empty dorm room two and three at a time to participate in the nightly Missionary Training Center floor prayer. By the time Amanda and her companion, Sister Baker, arrived, the room was nearly overflowing with young women dressed in their nightclothes, many hugging pillows to their chests. They found a spot in the corner where they could squeeze in between a girl in a Tigger nightshirt and another holding a teddy bear with the words "I'll be dreaming of you!" in huge red letters printed across its stomach.

Tomorrow morning Amanda was scheduled to leave the MTC and officially begin her service as a full-time missionary. A slight shudder ran through her body at the thought, and her chest filled with a suffocating sense of panic.

A hush fell over the room as one sister stood and took her place near the door. "We've completed a great week here at the MTC, and since it's Monday night, that means we have another district of sisters leaving tomorrow. Sister Anston and Sister Wright will be going to the California Santa Rosa Mission, and Sister Baker and Sister Kelly will be serving in the California San Jose Mission. We would like to invite each of our departing missionaries to come up and share her testimony before our floor prayer. Sister Anston, why don't you begin?"

Sister Anston, a shy young woman from Georgia, took her place at the front of the room. She had short, curly black hair, chocolate brown skin, and a quiet, shy way of speaking that made it difficult to understand what she was saying. Amanda tried to listen closely, but the feeling of her stomach muscles tightening with anxiety was distracting.

Ever since she was a child, the thought of standing up and bearing her testimony filled Amanda with feelings of fear and anxiety. As a teenager, she would watch the other young women in her ward stand and pour out their hearts, tears streaming down their cheeks to show the depth of their emotions. And though Amanda was certain that she had a testimony, she just couldn't bring herself to get up in front of other people without any preparation and try to explain how she felt.

Sister Anston, her Georgian accent sweet and rhythmic, finished her testimony, brushed a couple of tears off her cheek, and sat back down with the other sisters. Sister Wright took her place.

Sister Wright was twenty-six and a woman of straightforward speech. She was tall and slender and wore her hair pulled back in a tight bun.

"I wasn't sure about my decision to come on a mission," she said, picking at a tissue she held in her hands. "I'm older than most of you, and I wondered whether my time might be spent better in other ways."

A long pause followed, as if Sister Wright wasn't sure how to continue. Finally, and with great effort, the words came choking out. "But I know this is where I'm supposed to be."

The testimony was simple, almost childlike, and yet the response was immediate and the Holy Ghost could be felt in every corner of the room. The presence of the Spirit made Amanda's heart begin to pound, and she felt a knot of anxiety tying itself in her midsection.

It wasn't as if Amanda was afraid of public speaking. As an English lit major at BYU, she'd spent years writing up research papers and presenting them in front of other students and professors. One semester she'd helped teach a freshman English class. The difference was, on those occasions she was completely prepared. She knew what she would say and how she would say it. There was little chance for a mistaken word or an awkward silence. The few times she'd tried to bear her testimony, her mind would go blank, and any words she did manage to speak sounded mixed up and ill chosen. She always finished feeling foolish, and there was nothing in the world Amanda hated worse than feeling foolish.

Sister Baker squeezed Amanda's hand tightly for a moment before she rose to her feet. As the oldest of ten children, all born and raised in Price, Utah, Sister Baker had worked for over a year to save up enough money to go on this mission. She'd confessed the night before that tomorrow would be her first time on a plane and she was scared to death of the upcoming flight.

"I've wanted to go on a mission for as long as I can remember," Sister Baker began, smoothing her curly red hair back from her face. "I know that it won't be easy, but I'm so excited to have this opportunity. I feel like one of the stripling warriors ready to march forth in the Lord's cause."

Amanda's heart was beating faster. In a few minutes it would be her turn, and she had no idea what she was going to say. Even the silent prayer she offered did little to calm her fears.

"I know the gospel is true," continued Sister Baker. "And I can't wait to get out to San Jose and share my testimony with everyone who will listen. I say this in the name of Jesus Christ, amen."

Sister Baker smiled as she made her way back across the room. It seemed to Amanda that her companion glowed with an inner light—one that burned so brightly even her flesh couldn't contain it. She reached a hand down to Amanda and pulled her up. "Your turn," she whispered.

Amanda stood for a moment and then began to move unwillingly toward the front of the room. All around her the upturned faces of other sister missionaries showed anticipation. No doubt they expected her to share some great spiritual experiences she'd had during the last three weeks. Boy, would they be disappointed.

Amanda took a couple of deep breaths. She wished someone would pull the fire alarm outside in the hall and save her from this ordeal. But when no sirens began to wail, Amanda knew she had no choice.

"I am grateful for the opportunity," she began and then stopped. The words themselves were right, but to her they sounded insincere. She cleared her throat and tried again, this time adding more warmth and animation to her voice.

"I mean that I'm grateful to have the opportunity to serve . . ."

It didn't make any difference; her words still sounded contrived instead of heartfelt. Amanda could feel her face turning red. Her blood pounded so loudly in her ears that she couldn't think straight. Then words just began pouring out of her mouth almost of their own volition.

"I'm sorry, but I just don't know what to say to all of you. This has been the hardest three weeks of my life. I've tried so hard. I've done all the things they say we should do. I've read the Book of Mormon three times, twice before I came here and once more in the time since. I've studied all the lessons and memorized at least twenty-five scripture verses. I've read and prayed the way we're supposed to, and it just hasn't worked."

Amanda could see Sister Baker in the back, watching her with a look of concern. That should have been enough to stop this humiliating rush of speech, but Amanda couldn't stop. All the stress and frustration she'd bottled up would not be restrained.

"I've prayed that I could teach with the Spirit, and have the inspiration to know what I'm supposed to say, but I can't seem to feel it. I can repeat a scripture verse or quote *Preach My Gospel* without any problem, but when I have to come up with something on my own . . ." She shook her head. "I don't know. It just doesn't work."

By this time, all Amanda wanted to do was get out of the room and away from those staring eyes. She'd never felt so stupid in her life. Turning blindly, she grabbed the doorknob and pushed the door open, desperate to be alone with the feelings of hopelessness and despair that were ready to engulf her.

Amanda headed for the first place she could think of—the bathroom—and chose a stall at the end of the room. Locking the door after her, she stood with her forehead pressed against the cold metal panel and let the tears pour down her cheeks. The pain was not for tonight alone, but for all the frustration that had been steadily building up over the last three weeks.

"Sister Kelly? Sister Kelly, are you in here?"

It was Sister Baker. For one frantic second, Amanda considered jumping up on the toilet seat and hiding, but, of course, the idea was silly. In a few minutes floor prayer would be over, and the whole room would be full of chattering young women brushing their teeth, washing their faces, and preparing for bed.

Amanda slowly opened the stall door. "Over here," she said, trying to wipe the tears away before her companion noticed them.

"Are you okay? What happened?" Sister Baker asked.

"PMS probably." Amanda tried to sound light and airy, but to her dismay, her voice shook.

"This place is going to be mobbed in a few minutes. Let's get out of here so we can talk."

Sister Baker guided Amanda out of the swinging door and down to the room the two shared at the end of the hall. Once inside, Sister Baker propped her pillow behind her back and made herself comfortable at the end of the bed. "Talk to me, Sister Kelly."

Amanda turned away. "I think I pretty much said all there was to say in there."

"Come on now," Sister Baker said. "You've worked so hard, and you're going to be a great missionary. I don't understand why you're being so hard on yourself."

Amanda looked up. "It doesn't seem to matter how hard I work. I'm still totally unprepared to go out and teach. It just never seems to be enough."

"What do you mean by 'enough'?"

Amanda took a deep breath and tried to put her feelings into words. "I guess maybe it's a control issue or something. I don't like to find myself unprepared. At school I'd spend hours studying so that I felt confident to answer any question the teacher might ask."

Sister Baker nodded.

"But that doesn't work here. Too many subjects might come up for me to prepare for all of them or, even worse, spur of the moment times when you just need to know the right thing to say. I can't do it."

Sister Baker still appeared puzzled, so Amanda reached into her pocket, pulled out a folder paper, and handed it to her companion.

"What's this?" Sister Baker smoothed the crumpled page out on her lap.

"It's my testimony. The one I was supposed to give tonight. I was afraid to get up without CliffsNotes to try and say what I believe."

"It's a nice testimony."

"Thanks," Amanda said with a wry grin. "I think that's the part that bugs me most of all. I feel all that stuff. I know it's true. But when I try to stand up and say it, well, I end up looking and feeling dumb. I'm afraid that when I get in the field and come against something I haven't prepared for, I'm going to blow it."

"I don't believe you would blow it."

"But you don't know that for sure. There is so much at stake, and I've sacrificed too much to ruin it now."

"A mission is a sacrifice for all of us."

"You're right," Amanda said, trying to find the words to explain what she was feeling. "But for me, there is this added weight. Have you ever felt that there was someone you were supposed to find and convert while you were on your mission? That if you didn't or if you said the wrong thing or didn't say the right thing, you might be responsible for that mistake forever?" Amanda knew her words sounded a little dramatic, but she didn't know how else to explain it.

Sister Baker shifted her legs out from under her on the bed. "I can't say that I have," she said. "Do you believe there's someone out there you're supposed to find?"

"It's not just one person, more like a lost family I need to find."

"Lost, like how?" Sister Baker asked.

"I'm not sure. It's just a feeling I have, but it's so strong I called off my wedding to serve this mission."

Sister Baker stared at her. "You called off your wedding? We've been companions for three weeks and you never told me that?" The redhead sat forward on the bed. "I've known lots of girls who planned to go on missions, some even got their mission calls, and they turned them down to get married. I've never heard of anyone doing it the other way before. Did your parents go nuts?"

Amanda sat in her chair and put her elbows on the desk. "They weren't too happy, that's for sure, and they don't understand, but they're trying. My boyfriend, Jake, too. That's why I feel so terrible—all the people I'll let down if I can't make this work." Amanda put her hands to her temples. She could feel the beginnings of a headache.

Sister Baker sat quietly in thought for a few moments. "Do you want my advice?" she asked.

"Sure," Amanda said. She was already regretting the impulse that had caused her to share so much with her companion. She hugged herself and let her long hair fall down around her face.

"When I got my mission call, my dad told me, 'Taylor, you aren't going to convert anyone. You don't even have to try. Conversion is something that happens between the Lord and the investigator, but what you do need to do is be worthy to have the Holy Ghost help you.'"

"But it's the same problem!" Amanda said brushing her hair back with one hand. "I do everything I can think of to qualify myself for the help of the Spirit. If the MTC was like BYU I'd have a solid A. I don't understand why I can't make it work for me."

"Because you have to let go and trust the Spirit to be there. If we prepare and are willing to open our mouths and have faith, the Lord will tell us what to say."

"I don't know." Amanda frowned. "I hate feeling out of control like that."

"Me too, but I think this is all part of the plan. We have to learn to trust God more than we trust ourselves."

Amanda turned away and looked out the dorm window at the night sky beyond. It sounded so good just to let go and trust Heavenly Father. She just wasn't sure she could do it.

Chapter Two

August 5, 2008

Dear Amanda,

It's only been a few weeks since I said good-bye to you, and yet it feels like it's been two years. Hopefully the next seventeen months will go faster. I want you to know that I think you're going to be a great missionary, and I wouldn't take that away from you. Still, you might be interested to know that I put up a calendar just to mark off the days until you're back and we can pick up where we left off. In the meantime, I'll be cracking the books and thinking of you.

Love always,
Jake

The Salt Lake City airport was full of elders and sisters waiting to board the planes that would take them to their new mission fields. Amanda and Sister Baker had arrived more than two hours early. Now it was nine-fifty in the morning, and the two stood waiting at gate B12 for their ten-thirty flight. Amanda left for a moment to use the restroom and brush out her hair. When she came back, she found Sister Baker chatting with an older couple.

"So you see," she was saying, "that's how we know about Christ's visit to the Americas after His Resurrection."

Look at her jump right in there, Amanda thought as she sat down. *Sister Baker isn't going to have any trouble teaching the gospel.*

Amanda had been up since four that morning packing her suitcases in preparation to leave the training center. She'd tried on three different outfits searching for something to make her look more confident than she felt. Like the rest of the missionaries traveling that day, Amanda was anxious to get out of Utah and into her mission field. At the same time she still felt uneasy. *What if I can't do this?*

The couple left a few minutes later to catch their plane, and Sister Baker turned to Amanda. "Do we have time to go to the water fountain before we board? The doctor at the MTC gave me something to take before the flight to help me relax."

"If we hurry," Amanda said.

By the time the sisters boarded the plane, most of the other passengers had already taken their seats and the two girls had to hurry to find their places. Amanda was assigned the center seat. On her left by the window sat a middle-aged woman with black hair, olive skin, and fashionable glasses who was flipping through the airline magazine. She glanced up once as Amanda sat beside her before returning to her reading.

Sister Baker looked absolutely green as she sat in the aisle seat and fastened her seat belt. Amanda watched in sympathetic amusement as Sister Baker rechecked it twice, making sure the clasp was secure.

After a few minutes, the plane began moving slowly down the runway, increasing in speed until finally it began to lift into the air. Amanda never failed to appreciate the exhilaration of takeoff.

From the first time she'd stepped on a plane at the age of thirteen to attend a music competition, Amanda had enjoyed flying. And she recalled that the flight home was even more exhilarating with the knowledge that a first place trophy was packed away in her bags.

She reached into her pocket searching for a piece of gum and felt the envelope that contained Jake's most recent letter. The words had been encouraging, with only a hint of the longing he couldn't quite hide, and the thought of him watching the days pass like some lovesick BYU student waiting for her missionary made Amanda laugh. Only Jake could get away with something like that. He was like no other guy she'd ever met. That was the reason she started dating him in the first place.

* * *

It had been an unusually mild February afternoon during her first year at BYU, and she'd been sitting on a bench near the fine arts building enjoying the warmth of the day and reading. The sunlight cast a pale yellow hue on the pages of her book, and a soft breeze kept blowing her long hair down around her face. She pushed it back behind her ear for the third time when a shadow fell across the pages of the book. Looking up she saw a young man staring down at her, his face somewhat obscured by the sunlight shining through his rich reddish-auburn hair.

"*For Whom the Bell Tolls,* huh? Are you a Hemingway fan?" he'd asked.

"I liked *The Old Man and the Sea* better." She shaded her eyes and squinted up at him, her tone deliberately aloof. "I think it speaks more to the human condition."

It wasn't unusual for a male student on campus to try and pick up on her. Amanda's roommates said it was her slender build and golden blond hair that fascinated them. However, the minute they realized that underneath she had a brain and knew how to use it, the guys quickly disappeared.

"Yeah, I guess the symbolism is there," he said, seemingly oblivious to the arrogant tone in her voice. "But my problem is that I just don't agree with his whole view of life. It's so fatalistic, like Willy Loman in *Death of a Salesman.* I just refuse to believe that our existence is that bleak. I think life is what you make of it," he concluded and looked at her expectantly.

Amanda was so startled at his concise evaluation of Hemingway's work that she was barely able to stutter an intelligible, "Uh, yeah."

He smiled, tilting his head to one side, and she could see his deep blue eyes clearly. "My name is Jake Mitchell. May I sit down?" he asked.

She planned to say no—she always said no—and opened her mouth with that intent. Instead she found herself saying yes, and he sat beside her on the bench.

They talked for the next two hours—about books, philosophy, religion, and school. He seemed to have something intelligent to say about almost everything. She found his conversation clever, insightful, and often funny. By the time they reluctantly parted, he had her phone number and a date set up for the next weekend.

* * *

The plane lurched and Amanda forced her mind back to the present. Looking around, she noticed that the woman on her left was now staring idly out the window.

If I were Sister Baker, thought Amanda, glancing over at her companion who appeared to be asleep, *I would probably be talking to this woman about*

*the Church rather than daydreaming about my boyfriend. But of course, I'm not
Sister Baker.*

She didn't know why the idea of just letting go and talking to strangers about the Church scared her so badly. She'd always been a confident person, performing French horn solos since she was in the fifth grade. She'd easily overcome her stage fright, but this was much more difficult. Still, she was a missionary now, and she had the obligation to at least try.

The woman had removed her glasses and was cleaning them with a tissue.

All I need to do is open my mouth, and the Spirit should tell me what to say. It sounded easy, so why did she feel like a child standing at the edge of the high dive, trying to get up the courage to take that one last step? *Come on, Amanda, you can do this.*

She turned slightly in her seat. "How are you?" Amanda asked in a voice that sounded raspy and unsure.

It took the woman a moment to respond, as if Amanda's words had to penetrate deeply into her thoughts.

"Hi," she said finally, her eyes moving down to read the missionary name tag.

Think of something, think of something. Amanda cleared her throat. "Uh . . . Did you enjoy your stay in Utah?"

That was dumb. Maybe she lives in Utah.

"It was work more than pleasure, but I guess it was okay." The woman's tone was distant, but a smile played at the corners of her mouth, as if she sensed Amanda's nervousness.

"So what kind of work do you do?" Amanda hoped the question wouldn't seem too personal.

The woman answered readily. "The hair-care business. I own several salons in the South Bay area, and I was attending a national conference at the E Center. And you," she looked at Amanda's name plaque, "appear to be a Mormon missionary. Is that right, Sister Kelly?"

"That's right." Amanda was relieved that the woman had broached the subject. Maybe this was the Spirit's influence helping her to share the gospel.

"I'm Lyn, and if I understand correctly, you are leaving your home to teach about your church without any kind of pay whatsoever. Is that correct?"

Amanda, now on the receiving end of the questions, tried to answer as clearly as she could. "That's right. For the next eighteen months I'll be serving in the San Jose area sharing the gospel."

"Why?"

The question caught Amanda off guard. "Why what?" she asked.

"Why are you doing it?" Lyn watched Amanda closely.

This would be a real nice time for the Spirit to kick in with the right words for me to say. Amanda took a deep breath. "I guess because I want to share the message of Jesus Christ's Church with others and because Heavenly Father wants me to go."

Lyn laughed a little, but it wasn't a happy sound. "See, there is the main difference between us," she said, pointing one manicured finger at Amanda. "You believe in a God and I don't. You're how old? Twenty-four, twenty-five?"

"Twenty-two."

"Twenty-two, huh?" Lyn shook her head. "You know, when I was a child I used to believe in God too. My grandma told me Bible stories before she died, but by the time I was your age, I'd already seen enough of this world to know that if there was a God, He was just some impotent old man helplessly watching us destroy ourselves. You haven't seen much of life yet, I don't think, but you will, and then you'll realize the foolishness of believing in anything other than yourself."

Amanda drew back in her chair and stared at the woman beside her. "But God isn't like that," she said.

"Let me tell you about a side of life you've evidently never experienced," Lyn said with a look of grim determination on her face. "Imagine a girl growing up in a house where both of her parents drank constantly. Imagine her in bed at night listening to them beat each other up until one or both of them passed out and she could finally go to sleep."

Amanda shifted in her seat. "You know, you don't have to tell me this if you don't want to . . ."

"You need to know the way the world really works," Lyn said, turning slightly so she was facing Amanda.

Lyn explained how, as she got older, if she was around the house, her mom and dad would beat her as well. So she stayed away as much as she could. It wasn't long before she'd learned to escape through the bottle, just like her parents.

Lyn no longer seemed aware of Amanda. Instead she appeared to be lost in her memories, a haunted look in her eyes as she went on to recount how, at seventeen, she'd moved in with Will, a mechanic at a nearby garage. He was decent to her, despite her drinking. When he finally left her, he didn't know that she was pregnant with his child.

Lyn was breathing hard, as if the effort to tell her story had depleted her strength.

"It's not like Heavenly Father is responsible for . . . ." Amanda began, but Lyn interrupted her.

"Of course He's not responsible because He isn't there!" Her voice was loud enough to carry across the row. The man sitting in front turned around and glared at them between the seats.

Lyn spoke more quietly, but her tone held the same intensity. "It's just a story we tell ourselves so we don't feel so alone in the world."

"But we aren't alone." Amanda leaned toward her. "We all have some-one. You have your child, don't you?"

"What do you know about my baby girl?" Lyn lashed out, tears form-ing in her eyes.

Amanda recoiled as if she'd been slapped. "I'm sorry. I didn't mean to offend you." She watched uncomfortably as Lyn struggled to get her emo-tions under control.

"No, I'm sorry," the older woman apologized, her voice weary. "How could I expect you to understand?"

Amanda waited. She wondered if the child had died.

"I worked nights at a bar." Lyn's laugh was bitter. "Not a good place for an alcoholic and definitely not for a four-year-old. I didn't have the money for a babysitter, so I sometimes had to leave my baby alone at home sleep-ing. After a couple months, a neighbor called family services and reported me for neglect. My daughter was put into foster care."

Amanda found that she was holding her breath and forced herself to exhale.

"I went kind of crazy," Lyn continued. She ran her hand through her hair. "I tried to get her back, but they wouldn't even let me see my own child without some social worker spying on us. Every time I had to leave she would cry so hard she made herself sick.

"I went on this drinking binge for two weeks straight. It was pretty stu-pid, but she was my whole world and it hurt so bad. Finally, I couldn't take it anymore and I tried to kill myself."

Amanda stared in horror at the raw pain exposed on the other wom-an's face. She wanted to reach and touch Lyn's shoulder to somehow offer comfort, but there was anger in her face as well, and Amanda didn't dare move.

"They kept me in the hospital for a few weeks and then moved me to a rehab program. It was almost two years before I was finally able to kick the alcohol. Once I was sober, I tried to find my daughter, but the state had terminated my rights as a parent. They said that my little girl had been adopted and there was nothing more I could do."

Amanda murmured sympathetically, but she wasn't sure the other woman even heard her.

Lyn closed her eyes and took a couple of deep breaths. "I probably should have hired a lawyer and tried to fight it, but at the time I was too devastated to think straight. Tell me, Sister Kelly, how could a loving God let that happen?"

Amanda didn't know how to answer.

"Maybe if I'd lived a different kind of life, one like yours, I could make myself believe in some higher power," she said, her voice sounding wistful. "But it's too late now."

Amanda opened her mouth and then shut it, knowing there was nothing she could say.

Lyn seemed suddenly embarrassed. "I didn't mean to dump all this on you," she said. "It was a long time ago. I've been married and divorced twice since then. It's just that I want you to understand that not everyone believes in an all-loving God, and I hope that you'll respect the fact that I don't want to discuss religion with you." She reached over and patted Amanda's arm. "I wish you the best," she said before turning away to stare out the window.

Boy did I ever blow that one, Amanda thought to herself. *I opened my mouth and promptly stuck my foot in. I thought the Holy Ghost was supposed to help me know what to say.*

A deep feeling of depression settled over Amanda. *Would it have been better if I'd minded my own business and kept my mouth shut?* she wondered.

She looked back at the woman beside her. Lyn was still facing the window, but Amanda noticed that her shoulders were slumped and that she'd clenched her hands tightly together on her lap. The story Lyn told was tragic and heartbreaking. But what was worse, she'd had to go through it all without the knowledge of God and His mercy.

Pulling her scriptures from her purse, Amanda considered what she might have said in response to Lyn's questions and whether her words could have possibly penetrated all the anger and bitterness that had built up in the older woman's soul. She flipped through the pages of her quad, but nothing seemed to jump out, so she closed them again. Amanda felt a yearning within her heart to reach out, but she just didn't know how.

Father, she called silently into the heavens, *I need you. I don't know what to do to reach this daughter. Please send me an answer, help me to understand it, and let her feel the Spirit.*

For a moment there was nothing, no warm peaceful feeling, no answer, and then as clearly as if someone had spoken it in her ear, she heard the words: "Bear your testimony."

Amanda sat there in surprise. Had she imagined it, or had she really heard the answer?

Again the voice came into her mind: "Bear your testimony."

But I can't. She doesn't want to listen to me.

A third time the voice came to her: "Bear your testimony."

Amanda could feel her heart pounding, and her hands shook a little in her lap. She was scared, but she couldn't deny the answer. Preparing for the worst, she turned to the woman beside her.

"Lyn?"

"What?" she responded, her voice sharp.

Amanda took a deep breath. "I know you said you don't want to hear any more religious stuff, and I respect that," she hurried on, fearful that Lyn wouldn't let her finish. "But I need you to know that I don't just believe that Heavenly Father exists and that He loves us. I am convinced of it. I don't know why you had to go through so many awful things in your life, but I do know that you're His daughter and that He loves you and wants you to be happy. God can make such a difference in your life if you'd just let Him. I know it as surely as I know you're sitting here. I wanted you to understand that."

Amanda could feel the Spirit's presence between them. She'd done it! She'd opened her mouth and the right words had come. Lyn was silent as Amanda sat trying to catch her breath. Surely the woman could feel it too. For a few seconds Amanda felt as if she were on top of the world. Then Lyn spoke.

"I'm glad that you have your faith, but I don't think you have any right to force that belief on other people. You can preach till you're blue in the face, but you can't change the way I feel and that's all there is to it."

Amanda's euphoria caved in like a popped balloon. Her testimony meant nothing. Lyn hadn't felt a thing.

"Look, most people in the world aren't like me," Lyn said as if regretting the sharpness of her words. "What you're doing is kind of noble. If it will make you feel better, you can give me a brochure or something and then mark me off as a lost cause."

With a trembling hand Amanda fished into her purse, pulled out a pass-along card for the Book of Mormon, and handed it to Lyn. She was afraid to talk, afraid that her voice would crack or that the tears would come.

"Thanks." Lyn stuffed the card into her pocket and turned away.

The plane began its descent, and the San Jose area came into view. Amanda saw thousands of tiny houses, one next to another, divided by dark ribbons of road on the land below them.

The sight of her new mission field left Amanda with a feeling of dismay. The next seventeen months stretched out like an eternity in front of her. She wondered what would happen if she just stayed on the plane and insisted they take her back to Utah.

Will I ever be able to do this?

Chapter Three

August 13, 2008

Dearest Jake,

I've been here seven days and I'm still feeling a little lost. My trainer is a petite Italian girl from Newark, New Jersey, and she is so funny. She has this kind of nasal Jersey accent, and she can't say a word without using her hands. She's a good missionary, but boy is it hard to keep up with her.

We are assigned to the Sunnyvale Ward. It's kind of an interesting area. Subdivision after subdivision of matching stucco houses set right next to each other. At least it makes tracting easier.

I miss you so much, and I think about you a lot. It seems strange that you're only a few hundred miles away and yet it might as well be another planet! I know you'll do great at BYU. Remember how much I love you.

Love always,
Amanda

"So ANYWAY, WE KNOCKED ON this door, and it just opened. The door, I mean. I guess it hadn't been closed all the way. Sister Thompson and I looked at each other, wondering what we should do. We both felt like we needed to be at that house, but it didn't seem like anyone was home."

Amanda had only been in the mission for a week but had already learned that her trainer, Sister Ferrari, could talk nonstop for hours at a time.

"So, anyway," Sister Ferrari continued as they walked past a city park, "Thompson started yelling, 'Hello, anyone home?' and we heard this weird noise from the back of the house. I thought it was a cat or something. My companion called out again, but there was no answer.

"Sister Thompson wanted to go inside, but I thought she was crazy. I mean, if anyone came home and found us wandering through their house in this area, they'd shoot first and ask questions later, right? But she was senior, so what could I do?"

The two missionaries crossed a major intersection and turned left. Although they had the use of a perfectly good Toyota Corolla, Sister Ferrari preferred to save their gas allowance for trips over three miles.

"We walked into the hall, and as we passed the bathroom, we noticed this really, really old lady wearing a flannel nightgown lying on the floor next to the tub. She looked dead! Her eyes were shut, and she was so still."

"You're kidding!" Amanda said in amazement.

"No, it's the truth. As we got closer we could see her chest was moving up and down, so we called 911. Turns out she'd fallen down the night before after filling her cat's dish with water and had been lying there for over twelve hours, but the funny part happened when we went to visit her in the hospital the next day. She said she appreciated our help and that we were such nice young women, but she was Lutheran and didn't want us to visit her again."

"No! That didn't really happen, did it?" Amanda asked in amazement.

"Yes, it did. The things I could tell you about this mission. In a few months, nothing will amaze you."

That was already true. From the moment Amanda had arrived in San Jose, nothing had been what she'd expected. For one thing, her companion had entered her world like a short, dark-haired tornado.

"Sister Kelly! I'm Sister Ferrari, your trainer," she'd said when they met in the mission office, and before Amanda knew what was happening, her companion was hugging her tightly.

"You're just going to love our area. We have a great ward, and there's so much work to do."

Amanda quickly learned the truth of her words. Sister Ferrari kept them both so busy visiting less-active members and teaching that she didn't have time to think about her own shortcomings.

Her companion had moved on to another story involving a couple of elders and an Oreo-eating contest. "This one guy managed to down a full package of Oreos and a half gallon of milk in twenty minutes flat," she said, tossing up her hands. "Only an elder."

At last they arrived at their destination, the left side of a small duplex. A gentle breeze stirred a patch of yellow daisies that grew against the wall as Sister Ferrari moved toward a door thrown into shadows by the warm afternoon sun.

"You have to knock really loud." Sister Ferrari banged with all her might. "She's a little hard of hearing."

A tiny old lady with wispy white hair and slightly watery blue eyes answered. She greeted the sisters warmly, embracing them with thin, fragile arms.

"Eva, this is my new companion, Sister Kelly," Sister Ferrari said, speaking loudly. "Sister Kelly, meet Eva Emerson."

Eva peered up at Amanda. "Well, how nice, how nice. Please come in."

Amanda followed Sister Ferrari into the small apartment and sat down next to her on a gold velvet couch. The room smelled like a musty mixture of witch hazel and menthol vapor rub. Eva settled into a chair across from the sisters as a huge black cat sauntered into the room.

"Eva!" Sister Ferrari yelled. "Did you get a chance to look at the book we left you last time we were here?"

"That's nice, dear," Eva said, nodding like a bobble-head dog in the rear window of a car.

The cat made its way to Amanda and began rubbing against one of her legs. With a smooth fluid leap he landed squarely onto Amanda's lap and started kneading her legs with his massive paws.

"That's my baby, Midnight. I think he likes you," Eva said, clapping her hands like a delighted child.

Amanda stared at the animal in dismay. She'd always been allergic to animal dander, and just being in a home that had cats could make her eyes itch and her nose run.

Midnight finished kneading and had now settled heavily on Amanda's lap, his eyes shut, with a purr that sounded like a rusty lawnmower. She tried shifting slightly to dislodge Midnight, but the cat wouldn't budge. Already she could feel her eyes watering.

"We brought a movie to show you." Sister Ferrari slipped *The Lamb of God* video into Eva's VCR and turned the volume as loud as it would go. The little old lady continued to smile and nod.

Once the movie began, Sister Ferrari turned to Amanda. "I'll get him off," she whispered, reaching into her purse and pulling out a small bag of kitty treats.

"You carry cat food in your purse?" Amanda asked as she wiped the moisture from her left eye.

"Sure, and stickers for fussy kids, cough drops, wet wipes—all kinds of stuff."

Midnight opened his eyes and watched as Sister Ferrari held the treat close enough for him to smell, but far enough away that he couldn't quite reach it. He batted at the air a few times before finally pushing himself to his feet. Amanda winced as his claws dug into her thighs.

Her companion was ready, quickly tossing the morsel to the floor a few feet from where they were sitting. Midnight jumped after it, snatching the treat in his mouth and carrying it from the room without so much as a backward glance.

"Works every time." Sister Ferrari laughed.

They left fifteen minutes later after promising to come back soon.

Once they were out the door Amanda took a deep breath of fresh air before turning to her companion. "I thought we were never going to get out. My sinuses are killing me."

"I'm sorry. I didn't know you were allergic."

"It will pass now, but what I don't understand is why we are here in the first place. She's a sweet old lady, but it's evident she can't hear a word we say, and she slept through most of the movie."

Sister Ferrari met her gaze evenly. "Eva is ninety-seven years old, and the sister missionaries have been in her home almost every week for the past six months. She gets very lonely, and these visits mean a lot to her."

"I'm sure, but it seems to me that we are wasting our time," countered Amanda.

"She's a daughter of God, just like we are, and I know she feels our love and concern for her. She probably won't join the Church in this life, but once she gets on the other side, I feel pretty certain that she'll be receptive to the missionaries over there."

Amanda stared at her trainer in amazement. *Did she just tell me that we're preparing referrals for the spirit world missionaries?*

Before she could pursue the subject further, Sister Ferrari had already begun walking down the block, and Amanda was forced to run after her.

* * *

September 4, 2008

Dear Amanda,

I know it will feel a little weird for a while, being new in the mission and all. But just remember, every missionary started off as a greenie. Even your trainer.

It feels so good to be back in school. It's like I never left. It seems like the campus is full of freshmen this year, and some of them don't look like they're old enough to be out of high school.

I'm taking math, English, and psychology. Oh, and I signed up for a marriage and family relations institute class. Just want to be ready when you get home in sixteen months. But, hey, who's counting!

Love you,
Jake

Two weeks passed quickly, and Amanda soon became familiar with the area and comfortable with the daily routine. They studied, prayed, and put in hours of visits and tracting, but despite all their efforts, Amanda felt they weren't making much progress locating new investigators.

After giving the problem some thought, she spent all of her personal study time for the next two days pouring over maps of their area and making notations in a spiral-bound notebook. By the second day Sister Ferrari couldn't contain her curiosity any longer.

"What are you doing?" she asked.

Amanda glanced up and smiled. "Actually, it's almost ready. Sit down. I want to show you what I've come up with."

Sister Ferrari pulled up a chair, and Amanda slid the page in front of her. She'd divided the paper into sections filled with tiny neat print.

"Wow," Sister Ferrari said. "I never saw anyone who could write that small."

Amanda blushed. "At BYU, I used to organize my schedule on one sheet of paper. It helped me feel more in control of my life."

"I'll bet you did," Sister Ferrari said with a smile.

"Okay, I've gone over our area, and it appears that the highest concentration of people live here." Amanda leaned over the map and pointed to a portion that she'd highlighted in yellow.

"According to my calculations," she said, pulling out a notepad covered with figures, "in five hours of tracting we can reach a square mile of homes. If we're invited into one out of every fifteen and teach a forty-five-minute lesson, that should take us up to about eight hours."

Sister Ferrari leaned forward, resting her chin on her hand.

Amanda went on, her own excitement growing. "So if we start here and work our way down, we should average three to four new investigators a week and probably four to five baptisms a month. What do you think?"

"You've put a lot of time and energy into this," Sister Ferrari said hesitantly, "and it looks well thought out."

Amanda heard an odd note in her companion's voice. "You don't like it, do you?" she said, sitting back in her seat.

"I never said I didn't like it," Sister Ferrari corrected. "It's just that tracting isn't the most successful finding method. Still, you've put a lot of effort into this. Organization has never been a talent of mine, but it appears to be one of yours."

"It's just that I feel like we aren't teaching enough people, and I think this would maximize our efforts," Amanda said. "The more people we can contact the better our chances. It's a numbers game."

"A numbers game?" Sister Ferrari looked amused. "Okay, then, you are now our official tracting planner."

The first day of tracting proved uneventful, and all they could show for their efforts were sore feet, but Amanda wasn't going to give up. Eventually the averages would be on their side.

The following day wasn't much better. But on the third day, two young college students who lived above a dry-cleaning store invited them into their apartment.

Kirsten was a thin, earnest-looking young woman majoring in art at the local community college. Her boyfriend, Chad, an attractive young man with slightly almond-shaped brown eyes and the beginnings of a goatee, attended there as well, studying computer science. The room was furnished like most student apartments, littered with an odd assortment of mismatched furniture, books, and papers. Several rather good pencil drawings had been thumbtacked to the wall, and a large computer desk took up one side of the room.

"You know, Chad and I were just discussing religion the other day," Kirsten said once they'd all sat down. "We both believe in God. We even go to a Christian church down the block sometimes."

"Mostly Kirsten," Chad interjected.

"Yeah, that true," she agreed. "But what I was saying is that God doesn't seem real in our lives, and I'm starting to think that's wrong."

"Yes," agreed Sister Ferrari. "In today's world, we need a God who is aware of the challenges surrounding us. Sister Kelly and I can explain our beliefs about where we came from, why we're here, and where we're going after this life. If you'd like, we could come back and share this with you."

Turning Hearts 31

Chad sat forward, a look of concern on his face. "We're not searching for a religion, you understand."

"That's all right," continued Sister Ferrari. "It's a no-pressure kind of thing. We can teach you one lesson, and if you like, we can come back and do another. If not, that's okay too."

Chad stroked the hair on his chin with his right hand and didn't appear convinced.

"I do have some questions," Kirsten said. "And I'd really like to hear what you have to say."

Amanda could hardly contain her excitement. "We have the answers you've been looking for," she said firmly.

Once they'd set up an appointment for a few days later, the sisters said their good-byes and left.

"Can you believe it?" Amanda said as they walked down the stairs and onto the sidewalk. "That was so great."

"She does seem interested," Sister Ferrari said, shifting her backpack from one shoulder to the other. "But I don't know about him."

They headed left, back toward the parking garage where they'd left their car that morning. It was early afternoon, but already the shadows of the buildings around them had begun to lengthen.

"I'm not worried," Amanda said confidently. "I saw his type at school all the time. Really left-brained. I'm sure that once we lay the gospel out before him and he can see how logical it is, he'll come around."

"Maybe," said Sister Ferrari without much conviction. "The other tough part is going to be the law of chastity. But if they will read the Book of Mormon, pray, and are really sincere, the Lord can touch their hearts."

At the corner they stopped, waiting for the stoplight to change from red to green.

Could Kirsten and Chad be the family I'm looking for? Amanda wondered. *The girl certainly seems interested, but the guy is going to take some time. Still, it isn't hard to imagine them married and active in the Church—maybe with children and a temple sealing somewhere in the future.*

It was an exciting possibility, and Amanda was anxious to come back and teach them again.

* * *

In the upstairs apartment, Kirsten looked out the window, watching the two sister missionaries walking side by side down the street. There had been something about them, a feeling she couldn't put into words. She'd felt it the moment they'd arrived.

Chad stood behind her, looking over her shoulder. "You do realize who they are don't you? They're Mormons. That Utah religion where they have a bunch of wives and aren't allowed to drink or dance or anything."

"I'm sure that's not true," Kirsten answered slowly. "And I think it might be interesting to talk to them."

"Interesting? How can you go to college and still be so naive?"

She felt her anger rising. "Look, I didn't say I wanted to become a Mormon or anything. I just said I thought it was interesting. The girls are nice. I like them."

"Hey, don't get mad at me," he said taking her into his arms. "You can talk to anyone you like, but just don't expect me to waste my time. Unlike some people, I have a degree to earn."

* * *

Each Thursday morning the sisters attended a weekly meeting with the other missionaries in their district. Elder Haycock and Elder Greer were Spanish-language missionaries currently assigned to the El Camino Spanish Branch while Elder Brenner and his companion, Elder Larkin, worked in the Serra Park Young Single Adult Ward. District meetings were supposed to be used as a time to correlate work and exchange mission information as well as an opportunity to motivate and support one another.

Amanda sat on a folding metal chair in one of the stake center's classrooms unconsciously twisting a strand of hair around her finger. Over the past month she'd noticed that there was something about the spirit of these meetings that left her feeling frustrated and unhappy.

Elder Brenner, the district leader, stood with his back to the chalkboard reading off a sheet of notepaper he held in his hand. He was a stocky young man with thick dark hair, and Amanda wondered if he'd played high school football before coming on his mission.

"President Edwards wanted to remind all the missionaries not to hang out at members' homes after dinner appointments and to make sure we share a scripture and have a prayer with them before we leave."

Sister Ferrari made a note in her planner. "Do you and Larkin still have a baptism set for next Sunday?" she asked.

Brenner rubbed the back of his neck with his hand. "We did, but the guy had a setback, so we're going to have to reschedule. Is there any other news?"

No one spoke up so Brenner continued. "I had some inspiration for our district the other day. The assistants to the president were telling me that the most copies of the Book of Mormon ever placed in one month by a district in the San Jose mission is fifty-nine."

Elder Larkin scratched behind his ear while the other missionaries waited for Brenner to continue.

"That's a lot, I know, but I believe that our district could do better. I propose that we make it a goal to give out sixty-two copies of the Book of Mormon in the month of November."

"But that's like twenty for each companionship," Elder Greer said. "The most I've ever placed in one month was half that."

"If you aim for the stars you hit the top of the mountain," Brenner said, using a phrase that was often quoted in their mission. "But if you aim for the top of the mountain, you hit a tree." He shoved his left fist into his right hand for emphasis.

"What does that have to do with it?" Sister Ferrari asked.

Brenner beamed. "We have a chance at being a record-breaking district. Just think about how cool that would be . . ."

Sister Ferrari looked unconvinced.

"So Larkin and I are on board with this. Right comp?"

Elder Larkin nodded.

"Haycock, Greer? You two up for the challenge?"

The elders exchanged glances. "Yeah, I guess," Elder Greer said.

"Sisters, what do you say?"

"I'm just not sure this is a reasonable goal," Sister Ferrari said. "I don't want to feel like I'm ignoring my current investigators just to push a huge number of copies of the Book of Mormon for some contest."

"This wouldn't just be some contest. Giving out copies of the Book of Mormon is an important part of missionary work."

"True," Sister Ferrari countered, "but not for fame and glory."

Elder Brenner's eyes narrowed. "I don't understand why you have to fight every direction I give you. What is it about sisters?"

Sister Ferrari raised her chin up, giving her an air of defiance. "Elder, we're willing to give this idea of yours a try, but we're not going to commit to something we can't do."

Amanda shifted uncomfortably in her chair. By using the word *we*, her companion had placed them both in this antagonistic position.

"Maybe if you would exercise a little more faith instead of being so stubborn, we wouldn't be having this discussion," Brenner said, a flush of red creeping up his neck as he jabbed his finger toward them. "I don't know why they let girls serve missions in the first place."

Sister Ferrari's lips pressed together into a hard line. The tension in the room made Amanda's stomach twist, and she was relieved when Elder Larkin quickly stood and put a hand on his companion's shoulder. "We have an appointment soon. Probably time to wrap this up."

Brenner looked away from the sisters, but his face didn't regain its normal color throughout the closing song and brief closing prayer.

Amanda waited until the meeting was over and they'd reached their car before she spoke to her companion. "Why did you push him like that?"

"Brenner?" Sister Ferrari asked, opening the passenger door and sliding in. "I don't push; I push back. I just get so tired of his holier-than-thou attitude just because he has the priesthood and we don't."

"You think he thinks he's better than we are?" Amanda asked as she turned on the engine, letting it run for a moment.

"Well, don't you? And he's not the only one. I can't tell you how many elders I've run into who dislike female missionaries simply on principle. They think we're too emotional or that we came out on a mission because we couldn't find husbands at home and are now looking for them in the field."

Amanda pulled the car out of the parking lot. "I can't believe any of them would think that."

"Well, they do. Trust me on this." Sister Ferrari laughed dryly. "And it's crazy, really. I mean, who would go through all the trouble and hard work of serving a mission just to meet a bunch of nineteen-year-old guys?"

Amanda didn't respond as she eased into the flow of traffic.

"And speaking of future husbands," Sister Ferrari continued. "How is yours doing?"

The thought of Jake made Amanda smile. "He just started BYU a few weeks ago, and it sounds like it's keeping him pretty busy."

"Do you ever worry that he'll meet someone else while you're gone?"

Amanda chuckled. "Not a chance. We love each other too much, and besides, I already waited two years for him; he only has to wait eighteen months for me."

* * *

A few days later, when the sisters arrived at Kirsten's apartment for their next appointment, the young woman's face bore a strange expression when she answered the door, and she glanced over her shoulder twice before letting them in.

"Hi!" Amanda said in her most cheerful voice. "Is everything okay? If this is a bad time, we can come back later."

"Uh . . . no. No, this is fine." Kirsten looked over her shoulder again then lowered her voice. "I'm really sorry. But when I told him I was talking to missionaries, he insisted on meeting you."

"What are you talking about?" Amanda asked.

Kirsten simply shrugged her shoulders. "Come on in."

The young woman wasn't alone in the apartment. Behind her on the couch sat Chad and next to him a man in his early sixties. He had a long narrow face that seemed to slip into his neck without any sign of a chin. His eyes were small and dark, and his gray hair was thinning at the crown.

Kirsten cleared her throat. "Please sit down. This is Pastor Anderson."

Pastor Anderson was looking at them, a polite smile on his face that didn't quite make it to his eyes. Amanda wondered why he was there.

"It's nice to meet you," Sister Ferrari said.

He coughed. "Yes, well . . . Kirsten tells me she's thinking of studying religion with you Mormons," he said. "She's been in our congregation for a number of months, and I'm very fond of her . . . so naturally, I had a few concerns."

"Pastor Anderson, let me be frank," Sister Ferrari said. "I would be happy to explain our beliefs on any subject that you're interested in, but I don't want to get into a situation where a spirit of contention comes in."

"Of course, of course. I just want to clarify a few things," he said glancing at Chad. A slight smirk appeared on the young man's face. Kirsten, sitting off to one side, looked down at the floor.

His words seemed nice enough on the surface, Amanda thought, but there was a strange undercurrent she didn't understand. He picked up his Bible and began thumbing through it.

"First off, if I understand correctly, you believe that the Bible and your Book of Mormon teach the same things. Is that correct?"

Amanda glanced at her companion.

"Yes." Sister Ferrari sat on the edge of her seat as if preparing to jump up at any moment.

"Well, according to the Bible, in Acts, chapter eleven, verse twenty-six, it says that the followers of Christ were first called Christians in Antioch a few years after the death of Christ. I believe your Book of Mormon prophet, Alma, claims that the term was first used in 73 bc. How do you explain the contradiction?"

This was a concept Amanda had never heard before, and she wondered how a minister of another faith knew enough about the Book of Mormon to even ask a question like this.

Sister Ferrari let out a slow breath. "As we all know, neither the Book of Mormon nor the Bible was originally written in English, and *Christian* is an English word. When translating the Book of Mormon, *Christian* was the closest word Joseph Smith could find to match the meaning. However, even if both sides of the world had, in fact, used the same word, Luke, having no knowledge of the people living in the Americas, would have had no way of knowing whether a similar word was being used by them or not. According to his knowledge, what he wrote was correct."

Amanda looked at her companion in admiration. *I would never have known how to answer that.*

"Perhaps we ought to leave now," Sister Ferrari said, rising to her feet.

A dawning of understanding suddenly came to Amanda. These were not the questions of a person desiring to understand their beliefs. This man was looking to trip them up and make them look stupid in front of their investigator. She felt naive and a little foolish for not having realized it sooner.

Pastor Anderson was rapidly trying to regroup. "Well, let me ask you this. According to your beliefs, God has a body of flesh and bones. Yet, many times in the Book of Mormon, God is referred to as the Great Spirit. Can you explain that?" His voice was both challenging and smug.

"First of all, the Book of Mormon was referring to Jesus Christ, not God the Father—" Sister Ferrari began, but Pastor Anderson interrupted her.

"Then you admit that God is a spirit and does not have a body?"

"No, that's not what I was saying. I was trying to explain—" Sister Ferrari tried again, but the man wasn't listening.

"And in Hebrews, thirteen, verse eight, we learn that God is an unchanging God, and yet the Mormon God changes His mind all the time. First polygamy is good, then it's bad. First blacks can't hold the priesthood, then they can. How can you claim to believe in the Bible and yet not really agree with its teachings?"

Amanda was starting to get irritated. He should have the decency to let them respond to his charges.

Sister Ferrari turned toward the door and motioned for Amanda to do the same.

"It's evident to me that you're not interested in learning," Sister Ferrari said quietly. "We would love to discuss our beliefs with you, but, as I told you before, we are not interested in fighting. Good afternoon."

"You see, Kirsten?" Pastor Anderson said, his voice raised in pride. "They have no answers. They can't even explain what they believe. Just as the devils in the Bible could not stay in the presence of Christ, these workers of evil cannot remain in the light of truth."

Even though Sister Ferrari was heading for the door, Amanda could not let this pass.

She gave the man a cold stare. "Do you have a life?" Amanda asked him. "Don't you have anything better to do with your time than to tear down other people's beliefs?"

He looked back at her, and Amanda thought she could see a smile as he responded. "Young lady, if you choose to go to hell because you refuse to accept Christ and believe His word, well, that's one thing. But I will not allow you to pull a member of my flock down to be damned with you."

"How can you presume to call yourself a Christian?" Amanda countered. "I've never met anyone as rude as you are who claimed to believe in Christ."

"You know nothing of Christ," Pastor Anderson answered evenly. "You've been deceived, and you will pay dearly unless you repent."

Chad was grinning broadly now, and Amanda felt the adrenaline rush through her system. Sister Ferrari grabbed her arm and tried to drag her out, but Amanda was determined not to leave without having the last word. "I think you'll find out someday that it is you, not me, who needs to repent," she said before slamming the door shut behind her.

Amanda continued to vent her anger as they walked down the stairs. "What is that guy's problem? When he reads the Bible, doesn't he see how Christ behaved? That person is a modern-day Pharisee . . . or Sadducee . . . or something!"

They had reached the street now and were walking down the sidewalk. Sister Ferrari was uncharacteristically quiet.

"At least we were able to leave him with something to think about," Amanda ended uncertainly, not sure what to make of her companion's silence.

Sister Ferrari stopped and turned to look at Amanda. "Sister Kelly, what do you think you were doing in there?"

The response took her completely by surprise. "What do you mean? I was standing up for us . . . for the Church."

"You did nothing for us or for the Church in there today. You pulled us down to Pastor Anderson's level."

Amanda was forced to wait indignantly as a noisy bus passed by them before she could continue. "But we couldn't just sit there and not defend ourselves," she said once the street had quieted down. "Surely Heavenly Father—"

"This has nothing to do with Heavenly Father, and His Spirit was nowhere in that room. That was your will, not His. Let me ask you something. If we, who have the truth, will fight and threaten and argue like those that don't, how are our investigators ever supposed to feel the Spirit and tell the difference?"

Her words stuck Amanda with a force that took her breath away. Suddenly, all her anger and resentment were gone. She felt sick inside. "I didn't think about it that way," she said.

"Sister, no matter how much we know or how hard we work, if we don't have the Spirit with us, we're basically useless to the Lord."

Amanda looked down, guilty and embarrassed. Her companion's words stung.

"Hey." Sister Ferrari slipped her arm through Amanda's. "It's okay. We all go through this when we first come out. Did I ever tell you about the time I tried to take on four Jehovah's Witnesses in my first area?"

Chapter Four

October 29, 2008

Dear Jake,

I'm so proud of you. Brother Tetchler is a tough teacher, and getting a B+ on your first English research paper is a real achievement. There are rumors that he's only given out a half dozen A's in his whole career.

It doesn't look anything like fall here in Sunnyvale. The weather has cooled down, but the trees are still filled with leaves only just beginning to turn brown. I miss all the vibrant colors of autumn at home. However, the hills have changed from dead-weed brown to a lovely shade of green thanks to the rain we had last week, so that's something.

I also wanted to tell you not to spend all your time studying. Go out to some of the ward socials and have some fun. I don't want to come home to a study-a-holic boyfriend! I love you and I miss you more than I can say.

Lovingly yours,
Amanda

THE NEXT SIX WEEKS WENT by almost too quickly. Amanda was excited to see that her tracting method had begun to produce results. The sisters had taught a single woman who was baptized and added two more investigators to their teaching pool.

One morning after breakfast, Sister Ferrari pulled out the area map and laid it on the coffee table between them. "Did they ever teach you about spiritual tracting in the MTC?"

Amanda thought back. Her time at the Missionary Training Center seemed like another life, despite the fact that only a few months had passed since she'd left. "I don't think so," she said, raising her eyebrows. "It doesn't mean looking for more spirit-world missionary referrals, does it?"

"That's an idea," Sister Ferrari said thoughtfully, then laughed. "No, seriously. Spiritual tracting is when we pray for inspiration and then look at the map to see what area we feel drawn to work in. That's where the Spirit part comes in: you let the Holy Ghost guide you."

Amanda frowned. She'd become comfortable working systematically through an area, knowing where they were going and why. She didn't see any reason for change.

Sister Ferrari began by offering a prayer, and then she studied the map carefully. "This is the place I feel good about," she said, pointing to a couple of streets near a park. "We'll tract there for a while. Now it's your turn."

Amanda's frown deepened. "My turn? I thought this was your project."

Sister Ferrari smiled. "We work together, remember?"

"But how am I supposed to choose?"

"It's not rocket science, Sister Kelly," said her companion in amusement. "All you have to do is look at the map, and when you feel good about a place, show me and we'll go there."

Amanda stared hard at the web of crisscrossing streets on the map in front of her until they all blended into one solid mass. It wasn't working. She felt absolutely blank. Finally, in desperation, she shut her eyes and jabbed her finger onto the map. "There," she said tentatively, opening her eyes. "I choose there."

Sister Ferrari studied the location closely. "Okay, we'll check it out."

The first stop was the neighborhood that Sister Ferrari had chosen, made up of newly built duplexes and condos. No one answered at many of the houses, and of the few people they actually spoke to, no one wanted to hear the message the sisters had to share.

"This spiritual tracting doesn't seem all that different from the non-spiritual type," Amanda said. She'd gotten a blister on her right foot the day before, and it was beginning to sting. She reached down and tried to adjust the back of her shoe.

"Okay, so we haven't had much luck so far, but we did get to meet some interesting people," Sister Ferrari reminded her.

Amanda rolled her eyes. "Which one did you find the most interesting?" she asked. "My vote is for that born-again guy who kept slamming his Bible shut as he talked in detail about the hell that was awaiting us."

"Actually, I was more impressed with the palm reader who warned you to avoid dark men with beards," Sister Ferrari said, laughing.

They had just completed the fourth block in the subdivision and had turned onto the fifth. As they left the first door, a neighbor came out on her porch and called to them.

"You're Mormon missionaries, aren't you? I've been hoping you'd come by."

Amanda turned to Sister Ferrari in surprise. "Do you know her?"

"I don't think so," Sister Ferrari whispered back.

"You're an answer to prayer," the woman said, holding the door open. "Please, come in."

The woman introduced herself as Jenny Green. She admitted to being a member of the Church since she was a child but said she hadn't attended for many years.

Jenny motioned for the sisters to sit down as she walked over to a small brick fireplace at the front of the room. "My son, Robby," she said, picking up a photo of a ten-year-old boy in a baseball uniform off the mantel. "He was asking me about God the other day. You see, his grandfather passed away three months ago. It was hard on all of us, but especially on Robby. The two of them were very close. He asked me what happens to people after they die and if he'd ever see his grandfather again. I'd been thinking about that myself. I didn't know what to say."

She paused, her gaze resting tenderly on the boy's picture. "When I was Robby's age, I remember feeling that God loved me. I understood how His plan worked, but I guess I've forgotten a lot. Since that conversation I've been thinking it was time that Robby and I had more religion in our lives. I just haven't been sure how to start."

Amanda listened in amazement as the Spirit filled the room. If they'd continued her systematic tracting, it would have been months before they'd worked their way up to this particular part of town. Yet her companion had felt inspired to come here today.

"The chapel isn't far," Sister Ferrari said. "It's a great ward with a lot of kids, and we would love to have you come on Sunday."

Jenny stood, wrote the time on her wall calendar, and circled the day for emphasis. "Great," she said. "I'll be there."

They visited a while longer, and the sisters arranged to come back and teach her son the lessons later that week. As they got up to leave, Jenny hugged them both. "I'm so glad you came!"

Once the door closed behind them, Amanda immediately turned to her companion. "Wow, that was incredible! Is it always like this?"

Sister Ferrari shook her head. "Not always, of course, but it's great when it is."

A small leaf blew down from a nearby tree and landed in Amanda's hair. She pulled it out carefully, letting it drop to the ground.

Sister Ferrari continued. "I'm sure there is merit in the idea that the more people we contact the greater the chances for finding people, but I've often found that it's not really about the numbers. It's about following the Spirit."

"Point taken," Amanda said with a grin. "I wonder what we'll find in the area I chose."

Fifteen minutes later the sisters pulled up in front of a broken-down, deserted brick building across the street from an empty lot. A cat jumped out of a dumpster. A number of homeless people wandered the street, and the faint odor of stale urine drifted in the air.

"The sisters aren't allowed to teach the homeless," Sister Ferrari said as she hit the lock button on the car door. "There were some problems a while ago, and now only the elders can teach them. Even they don't, unless the Spirit directs."

As Amanda stared out the window in dismay, Sister Ferrari placed a comforting hand on her shoulder. "It's okay. This morning was special. It doesn't always work out that way."

But Amanda knew what the difference was. Her companion had felt the Spirit and followed it. Amanda hadn't felt anything. She'd just guessed.

A feeling of depression settled over her as Sister Ferrari drove back to their apartment. *I don't understand. Why is this so hard for me?*

* * *

That evening, as Sister Ferrari changed into her pajamas, Amanda sat on her own bed with her feet curled up under her. "I can't figure it out," she said. "No matter how hard I try, I can't seem to get it. Sometimes I feel the Spirit so strong while we're teaching or when I'm reading the scriptures. But when it comes to something important like knowing where to tract or what to say to a tough question, I just can't seem to connect."

Sister Ferrari ran a brush through her hair. "There must have been times in your life when you've been guided to do things."

"I guess. I mean, I've felt good about going to BYU and majoring in English lit, but I don't know if that's the same thing."

"What about coming on this mission?" Sister Ferrari asked. "Something must have motivated you."

Amanda nodded. There had been something. A feeling so strong that no matter how hard she tried she couldn't ignore it.

* * *

November 8, 2008

Dear Amanda,

Just finished up midterms. I think I did okay, but this last stretch of semester is going to be tough. I took your advice and started going to some of my student ward activities. It seems I belong to a family home evening group and didn't even know it. I've also been playing basketball once a week with some of the guys in the elders quorum.

I'll be driving home to Idaho Falls in a couple of weeks for Thanksgiving. Two girls from my apartment complex who live in the area are coming along too. Where are you spending Thanksgiving? Wish it was with me!

Love you lots,
Jake

* * *

Amanda sat with the other missionaries in the district meeting listening to the mission announcements. Once he'd finished with them, Brenner moved on to the Book of Mormon challenge.

"So, Elders and Sisters, we are eleven days into November, and I'm sure we are all anxious to find out how many copies of the Book of Mormon we've given out. Elder Larkin and I have given out five." He wrote the number five on the chalkboard. "Elder Greer?"

Greer wiggled in his seat. "Haycock and I have given out . . ." He stopped and cleared his throat. "Uh, three."

Brenner lowered his eyebrows as he wrote the number three below the five. "I guess three is better than nothing, but you'll have to work harder next week. We each need to give out five a week to make our goal."

"Sisters?" he said.

Sister Ferrari looked up from her planner. "We have decided to abstain from this activity."

"You what?" Brenner asked.

"I don't think this is a good use of our time." Sister Ferrari met the angry eyes of their district leader. "So we will not be participating."

Brenner shook his head, and Amanda could see his fists clenching and unclenching at his side. "Ferrari," he bit out, "this is a district activity, and we need everyone's support to make our goal. You can't just refuse."

"I can and I am."

Amanda wanted to sink into the floor and disappear. She knew that Sister Ferrari had been less than enthusiastic about beating the district record, but this was the first time she'd heard her companion flatly refuse to be involved.

Brenner clenched his teeth. When at last he spoke, it was in a low, tight voice. "I think you need to pray about this again," he said. "Perhaps by next week you'll have more faith than you do now."

Sister Ferrari widened her eyes but didn't respond, and Amanda sighed. This was going to be a long month.

* * *

Kirsten had been taking the lessons steadily for two months, and since she'd called to apologize after their visit with the pastor, she was progressing well. She'd even attended church a few times and was talking about getting baptized at the end of the month. Unfortunately, Chad refused to participate in their discussions. He made a point of being out of the house or in another room every time they came.

"I'm making you a traditional Swedish meal," Kirsten said, motioning for the sisters to take a seat on the couch. "My mom was born in Sweden, and some of my relatives still live there."

"I didn't know that," Amanda said.

"Yeah. She went to school in the United States and then met my dad and married him, so I was born here."

"Have you ever been back?" Sister Ferrari asked.

"Only once when I was a child. My mother always talks about how beautiful it is, and she taught me how to cook all the dishes my grandmother had taught her. I'm making Gravad Lax." She glanced at the sisters and raised her eyebrows. "Cured raw salmon."

"Really?" Amanda said. "Are you sure that's safe?"

Kirsten laughed. "Not only is it safe, but it's delicious. The salmon is sliced real thin and served over crackers with a tangy dill and sweet mustard sauce. We're eating it with stewed potatoes."

Sister Ferrari looked at Amanda and shrugged her shoulders. "I'm not really much of a fish eater," she said.

"At least try it. Then if you want, I'll make you a ham sandwich," Kirsten promised.

The cured salmon tasted better than Amanda had expected, although she silently determined that this was one of those times in life where once was definitely enough.

After they finished eating, Kirsten brought out a tray of saffron-flavored sweet biscuits studded with raisins, and three cups of hot cocoa. "Normally we'd eat these with a sweet, fruity coffee," she said.

Amanda smiled. When they'd taught Kirsten the word of wisdom, she'd admitted that she never smoked and wasn't much of a drinker, but coffee would be tough. Sweden was one of the top coffee-drinking countries in the world, she told them, and so her mother had started her on it when she was a young child. But Kirsten agreed to try and give it up.

"How is Chad doing?" Amanda asked.

"Busy as usual. He has a bunch of projects to finish up before finals start next month, so I don't get to see much of him."

"I know how that is," Amanda said.

"Do you have a boyfriend?" Kirsten asked. "I mean, of course you probably do. I just thought with you being on your mission and all . . ."

Amanda laughed. "I do have a boyfriend and he's a great guy." She opened her wallet and pulled out a snapshot of Jake. In the photo his head was tilted to one side, the way it always did when he smiled. His hair looked unusually red in the studio lighting, and his eyes held the same look as when he gazed at her in person.

Kirsten took the photo and studied it. "He's cute. Is he back in Utah?"

"Yes. He's going to school, and when I get home we're going to get married in the Jordan River Temple."

Kirsten looked up. "What is the Jordan River Temple?"

They'd been planning on teaching Kirsten about eternal marriage and the law of chastity tonight. And, as was often the case, the Spirit had provided the perfect lead-in.

"Temples are different than regular chapels," Sister Ferrari began. "In them we do work and make covenants that will last forever."

Kirsten listened with interest as the sisters explained the purpose of temples. She was intrigued with the idea of baptisms for the dead. "I know this may sound strange," she said, "but ever since I was a little girl, I've had this strong desire to know more about my family line. My grandma would tell me stories about her parents, and sometimes I could swear that they were standing right there in the room with us, just out of sight."

"That's not strange at all," Sister Ferrari said. "In the Doctrine and Covenants we are told that in the last days the hearts of the children will turn to the fathers. And if you check out the Internet sometime, there are millions of sites dedicated to family research, which goes to show how true that prophecy turned out to be."

Amanda could feel the Spirit in the room, and she could see a brightness and a light in Kirsten's face.

"I could seal my great-grandparents to each other forever?" Kirsten asked.

"Yes, and their children too," Amanda said.

"This seems so right." Kirsten grinned broadly. "Like something I always knew and just forgot."

"And when you're ready," Amanda said, "you could be sealed in the temple to your own husband."

Kirsten blushed. "I'm in no hurry for that."

Amanda and her companion exchanged glances, and then Sister Ferrari began teaching about the law of chastity. As she listened, Kirsten's brow began to furrow.

"So what you're saying is," said Kirsten, "that in order to join the Church I have to marry Chad?"

"That's one option," Amanda said. "Or you'll need to live in separate apartments and refrain from physical intimacy until you are married."

Kirsten bit her lower lip, looking uncertain.

Sister Ferrari leaned forward. "Heavenly Father considers sexual relations between a man and a woman a sacred thing. And He commands us to wait to share in these experiences until we have made the legal and moral commitments that come with marriage."

Kirsten shook her head again. "I just don't know."

"Can you feel the Spirit?" Amanda asked.

Kirsten tipped her head to one side. "I guess."

"And what is it telling you?"

Kirsten closed her eyes as she spoke. "I understand what you're saying and why you believe that. It's just that I don't know if I can do it. I've got to think about it some more and talk to Chad."

"Why don't we go now." Sister Ferrari stood up. "You pray about it and then talk to Chad. We can come back in a couple of days if you'd like."

"Yes," Kirsten said, standing too. "I think that's a good idea."

* * *

The apartment was quiet after the sister missionaries' departure, and Kirsten stood at the bathroom mirror staring at her reflection, thinking about what the sisters had said.

She did love Chad, and they had talked about marriage once or twice over the past couple of years. But the thought of getting married now seemed so rushed and artificial. Still, the idea of leaving him was out of the question. He was a terrific guy and her best friend. Kirsten knew from experience that finding someone like Chad wasn't easy.

On the other hand, when she read the Book of Mormon and sat in church with the sister missionaries, she'd felt these amazing feelings. Feelings that told her that the things she was learning were true.

How was she supposed to choose between the man she loved and the new faith she was discovering?

* * *

"Look, I don't want to get married, and there's no point in discussing the issue anymore," Chad said.

Kirsten had waited up until Chad was home from his evening class then broached the subject of marriage. His strong opposition to the idea surprised her.

Kirsten could feel her eyes tearing up. "So what? You don't love me enough to marry me?" she asked.

Chad let out a long, frustrated sigh and then reached over and pulled her down to sit beside him on the couch. "You know that's not it. I love you with all my heart. It's just that I don't want to get married, and I don't understand why you think it's so important. It's just a piece of paper that the government can hold over our heads. I won't love you any more or be any more faithful with some expensive religious ceremony than I do now."

"I know," Kirsten said. "It's just that the sisters said that living this way is a sin and that in order to be baptized, we have to get married or stop, you know, being together."

Chad jumped up from the couch and paced angrily around the room. "I can't believe you are letting some religious cult mess with your mind like this. I love you and you love me and there is nothing wrong with our being together. How can you even want to be a part of some organization that makes you feel so guilty?"

Kirsten was crying in earnest now. "You don't understand. You wouldn't even listen. They have this place called a temple, and in it they can seal families together forever. Even people who have already died. Do you know what that means?"

"Temples? Do you know anything about those Mormon temples?" he asked, reaching for her hand and pulling her up off the couch. "Let me show you what they won't tell you about those temples."

She followed him to the computer where he sat down and punched in a few buttons on the keyboard. "I've been doing a little research on those Mormons and look what I've found."

Kirsten stared in dismay as one site after another opened, showing men and women dressed in strange clothing. Others showed long cotton underwear purportedly worn by Mormons who had gone to the temple. "They have strange and secretive meetings there, and no one outside of their religion is allowed to enter and see what really goes on."

"They said it was sacred," Kirsten said doubtfully. "But they didn't say anything about this stuff."

"Of course they didn't. They wouldn't." He stood up to face her. "Kirsten, I love you, and if you want to join these people, then go ahead. But you can't possibly expect me to change the way I live to accommodate their strange rules and rituals."

Kirsten put her hands to her face. "But it felt so good, and they said it was the Spirit."

Chad caressed her hair with his hand. "They got you all emotional. It could happen to anyone. But think about it. Doesn't the whole thing sound just a little too weird?"

She leaned in and rested her head on his shoulder. "I don't know what to think anymore."

* * *

The sisters had tracted all morning and missed lunch to teach a part-member family. When they were finished, they'd headed for Kirsten's house for their appointment, only to find that, for the first time, she wasn't there to meet with them. They'd then tried to find an inactive family in the late afternoon but couldn't find the house and later ate a burned meat loaf dinner at a dinner appointment with a member family. That evening they'd attended a ward missionary correlation meeting and then spoke to a group of Beehives who were more interested in talking to each other than in listening to what the sisters had to say.

"I'm starved and my feet are killing me," said Amanda, collapsing onto the couch once they were finally back at their apartment. She rubbed the sole of her left foot with her hand.

"Me too." Sister Ferrari headed into the kitchen. "I think this might be the right time for a little sister missionary S and S."

"I've heard of R and R, but what's S and S?"

"Soak and splurge," she said, pulling two beat-up plastic bins out from under the kitchen sink. "Can you get me the jar of pink bath salts in the bathroom?"

By the time Amanda returned with the jar and came back to the kitchen, Sister Ferrari had filled both bins with steaming hot water and was taking two pints of Ben and Jerry's ice cream from the freezer.

Ten minutes later, they were both sprawled out on the couch in the living room, their sore, bare feet soaking in rose-scented water and their faces smeared with brown mudlike face masks, eating spoonfuls of rich, decadent ice cream.

"Feel better?"

"I'm getting there," Amanda said, leaning her head against the back of the couch. She could feel her muscles relaxing as the warm water soothed her aching feet.

"What was the hardest thing you had to give up to come on a mission?" asked Sister Ferrari as she closed her eyes and savored a creamy spoonful of ice cream.

Amanda considered the question. She missed Jake, but it really hadn't been hard to put off the responsibilities of marriage. She did miss her family, but, since she'd lived away from home in an apartment near BYU for years now, the separation wasn't that difficult either. So far, the lack of privacy hadn't been a problem, and she actually enjoyed the highly structured mission environment. "I think what I miss most is the intellectual stimulation I had in college," she said at last.

"Intellectual stimulation?" Sister Ferrari nearly choked on her ice cream. "I thought you were going to say something normal . . . like, jeans . . . well, not jeans. I can't imagine you in anything that isn't tailored and pressed."

"I wear jeans sometimes," Amanda said. "I mean, I've worn them before."

"My point exactly," Sister Ferrari continued. "Or you might have said 'music in the car' or something. But 'intellectual stimulation'?"

Amanda laughed. "I miss being able to read great literature and being exposed to new thoughts and ideas. That's why I chose an English major. You read, say, *Pride and Prejudice* or *Grapes of Wrath,* and on the surface you find a good story with interesting characters. As you probe deeper, you find the art and poetry in the author's style. They use words like a painter uses color to influence and move the viewer. Delve further down, and you find the subtle messages and ideas that the writer wants to get across. These are all wrapped together using plot twists, characterization, and dialogue so that the readers don't even know that they're swallowing the pill until it's down."

"Wow." Sister Ferrari began to laugh.

"That's all right. I know it's different. My own father thinks I'm nuts."

"No, I'm not laughing at you. I'm laughing at myself. I was thinking that what I miss most is Taylor Ham."

"Taylor Ham?" Amanda stared at her. "What is Taylor Ham?"

"Basically it's a chopped and seasoned pork roll. My mom used to fry it for breakfast all the time. If you come out to visit me in New Jersey after your mission, I'll make you some."

Amanda took another spoonful of ice cream. It was hard to imagine Sister Ferrari as anything but a missionary. The fact that she had another life outside of their companionship seemed almost unreal.

"So," Amanda asked, glancing at the phone, "what are we going to do about our DL? He'll be making his nightly check-in call soon, and he's going to ask us about the Book of Mormon thing again."

"Brenner is just going to have to back off," Sister Ferrari said. "It's not like he can force us to do anything no matter how much he bullies."

"I don't think it's about pulling rank," Amanda responded. "He says we aren't supporting him, and I think he has a point."

"But he's wrong. Brenner is all about numbers and brownnosing the president. You and I know that isn't what missionary work is all about. How can we possibly support him?"

Amanda turned toward her companion on the couch. "So what your saying is we get to pick and choose what counsel to follow and what not to?"

Sister Ferrari stood up. "It's getting late, and I need to wash this stuff off my face. You take the call tonight."

Chapter Five

"THIS IS THE THIRD TIME today that I've called and there still isn't any answer," Amanda said. "Where could she be?"

For two days now, the sisters had tried to reach Kirsten, but their calls went unanswered, and no one opened when they knocked on her door.

"I don't know, but we just have to keep trying," Sister Ferrari answered.

They hadn't spoken to Kirsten since the night they'd explained the law of chastity, and Amanda feared that their investigator was having second thoughts. Still, until they could talk to her face-to-face and find out what was going on, there was little they could do. Amanda was frustrated and spent much of her personal prayer time pleading with the Lord to help them reach Kirsten.

To make matters worse, she hadn't heard from Jake in over a week. For the past three months Jake had written every Sunday night like clockwork, and by Tuesday or Wednesday Amanda would find his letter in her mailbox. But this week nothing had arrived. She knew that finals were coming up and he was bound to be busy studying for them. There was no reason to feel disappointed, but still, it added to the general discontent she was already feeling.

As the sisters arrived at the stake center for the district meeting, Amanda's mood was as dark as the storm clouds that had gathered in the November sky. The weatherman had predicted rain showers off and on throughout the day, and Amanda had brought along her umbrella just in case.

The other missionaries were already seated in the classroom when she and Sister Ferrari entered, and Elder Brenner looked at them coolly. "A little late, Sisters. Let's try and make it on time next week."

"Sorry," Amanda quickly said before her companion could respond.

The opening song and prayer did little to lighten the mood, and even the announcements seemed to increase the pressure. "Bishop Cook and his wife from the YSA ward have invited us all over to their house for Thanksgiving dinner next week," he said. "This will take the place of our regular monthly district activity."

Amanda had forgotten all about Thanksgiving. Her thoughts drifted back to the turkey feasts of years past. This would be her first holiday away from home, and the thought made her a little homesick.

Brenner continued. "We are at the three-week point, and for those of you who chose to participate in the district challenge," he looked directly at Sister Ferrari, "we are up to thirty copies of the Book of Mormon so far. If we can give out thirty-two more in the next two weeks, we will beat the record. We can do it elders, even without the sisters' help."

"How long are you going to keep this up?" Sister Ferrari asked with a frown. "Just because we don't care about beating some stupid record doesn't give you the right to criticize us."

"Some stupid record? I hate to tell you, but this is what missionary work is all about, Sister," responded Brenner. "It's hard and takes sacrifice, and if you aren't up to the challenge then you don't have any business getting in the way of those of us who want to work."

"Are you accusing us of not working? Because if you are . . ." Sister Ferrari began, but Brenner didn't let her finish.

"You don't know the first thing about hard work," he said, "because if you did . . ."

They were both yelling at one another now, and Amanda couldn't take it any longer. She jumped from her chair. "Stop it! Both of you."

Sister Ferrari and Elder Brenner turned to her in surprise, silenced by her outburst.

"You," she said, pointing to Brenner. "Missionary work is not about numbers. It's about people. We don't sell cars, and there are no top salesmen here. We share the gospel, and we do it one person at a time."

A slight smirk appeared on Sister Ferrari's face, which disappeared as Amanda turned on her. "And you have to get rid of that pride. Elder Brenner is our priesthood leader, and we need to be obedient all the time, not just when it's convenient."

Amanda continued. "We are servants of the Lord, and we aren't going to accomplish anything if we keep fighting among ourselves. I don't see how it matters whether we are sisters or elders. We are all missionaries representing the Savior, and we need to start acting like it."

With her temper spent, Amanda began to feel foolish. While the other missionaries watched in surprise, she turned and left the room. She walked quickly down the hall. Behind her, she could hear footsteps. Probably her companion, ready to chew her out big-time.

What was I doing? Amanda thought as she walked out into the rainy parking lot, not even bothering to put up her umbrella. *The elders are sure to think I'm crazy, and Sister Ferrari will never speak to me again.*

She got into the car and glanced over at Sister Ferrari, who slid into the passenger side, her eyes staring fixedly out the front window. They drove back to their apartment without saying a word. Only the soft swish of the windshield wipers moving back and forth across the windshield broke the tense silence.

Once they arrived home, Sister Ferrari didn't attempt to get out of the car. Amanda followed her lead, leaving her seat belt buckled and staring at the soggy bushes in the apartment parking lot.

"Sister Ferrari, I'm sorry . . ." she began, but her companion cut her off.

"Don't you dare apologize. You were completely right and I was wrong. I have been behaving badly, and I needed some humbling."

Amanda looked over at her companion, but Sister Ferrari was staring at the ground, her fingers twisting the strap of her purse that sat on her lap.

"And I want you to know how proud I am of you," continued Sister Ferrari. "You stopped acting like a scared greenie, and you actually spoke your mind. You followed the Spirit and did what needed to be done."

"I don't know about that," Amanda said. "I doubt losing my cool was exactly how the Spirit would have directed me."

"Okay, well, maybe not, but your point was valid, and I know you've been trying to get that across to me for a while. I'm sorry I didn't listen."

Amanda smiled. "So we're okay?"

"Oh, definitely." Sister Ferrari's eyes met Amanda's, but she still looked unhappy. "I think you had better start the car. We have to go back to our district meeting."

"Are you serious?" Amanda asked as her heart began to beat faster. The thought of facing all those elders again made her feel a little shaky.

"Unfortunately, yes. I have some repenting to do."

Throughout the drive, Amanda hoped against hope that the elders had closed their meeting early and left, but as they drove into the parking lot, both cars were still there. The rain had stopped, but the sisters had to carefully make their way around several puddles to get back to the building.

Amanda caught a glimpse of herself mirrored in the door. Her hair hung limply to her shoulders, the dampness having removed all of the curl.

Her makeup was smudged, and there was a large water stain across her skirt where she'd brushed up against the fender of the car.

Any shred of self-respect she might have clung to disappeared like her reflection as the door opened and the sisters walked in. As they made their way down the hall, they could hear the sound of unaccompanied male voices singing "Onward Christian Soldiers" with a noticeable lack of enthusiasm.

They were halfway through the third verse when the sisters' entrance effectively ended the song altogether.

Amanda stayed near the door, one hand on the jamb, the other gripping the strap of her purse. Sister Ferrari moved farther in and stood in front of Elder Brenner, who was watching her, his face expressionless.

"I want to say that I'm sorry," Sister Ferrari said. "I was way out of line. I didn't give you the support and respect you deserve and, again, I'm really sorry. I hope that you can forgive me, and I want you to know that Sister Kelly and I will be working hard the rest of the month to help the district meet the Book of Mormon goal."

The other elders had dropped their eyes to the ground, but Amanda thought she could discern a slight smile on Elder Larkin's face. For some reason, it made her feel a little better.

Elder Brenner stood up and shoved his hands into his pocket. He shifted from one foot to the other. "Yeah, okay. And I guess my idea might have come across sounding a little pushy. I just want to show the mission president, you know, that I can do this."

"I know," Sister Ferrari said. "And getting copies of the Book of Mormon out is always a good idea. I just have this thing about people telling me I have to do stuff."

Now Amanda was smiling.

"We were just about ready to pray," mumbled Brenner, "if you want to stay."

In response, both sisters folded their arms.

Once the prayer was over, the missionaries headed back down the hall toward the parking lot. As they walked, Elder Larkin pulled Amanda aside. "I've wanted to say that to him for months," he confessed. "Both his older brothers were APs on their missions, and the guy is scared he'll get passed over and have to go home as a lowly district leader or something. He's always trying to do stuff to be noticed."

Amanda saw Brenner in a whole new light. "That's got to be a lot of pressure on him."

"Yeah," Larkin agreed. "Sisters are lucky that they don't have to worry about that stuff."

Amanda couldn't agree more.

* * *

November 23, 2008

Dear Amanda,

Sorry about taking so long to get back to you. It's been a really busy few weeks. I had a term paper and two research projects to get in by the twenty-first. I made it, but I was up the whole night before finishing up. Diane, one of my family home evening sisters, and her roommates came by around midnight with some sandwiches and chocolate chip cookies. Talk about a lifesaver.

Well, I better get back to the books. I know you are working hard, and I miss and love you. Take care and I'll write a longer letter next week. I promise!

Love,
Jake

It was a Tuesday afternoon when Kirsten finally answered her door and let the sisters in. Over two weeks had gone by since they'd last visited with the young woman, and the change in Kirsten's manner toward them was marked. She kept her arms folded across her chest and didn't invite them to sit down. Instead, the three women stood in the small entryway.

Kirsten began. "Look, I'm sorry, but I don't want to meet with you anymore. You told me we would stop whenever I wanted to, and I want to stop now."

"Of course," Sister Ferrari said. "But do you mind if I ask why? You were so excited the last time we talked with you."

Amanda couldn't believe it. She'd grown to love and respect Kirsten. This cold distance was almost more than she could bear.

"It's a waste of time," Kirsten said. "I don't believe any of the things you told me, and I don't want to listen anymore."

"How can you say that? You felt the Spirit. I know you did." The words burst out of Amanda. "You can't turn your back on that, can you?"

Kirsten shook her head and turned away. "I don't know what I felt, but whatever it was, I know it's not for me. I think you'd better leave now."

With tears in her eyes, Amanda followed her companion out the door and heard it shut behind them. She felt enveloped by sadness. "I don't understand," she said. "I really thought she'd felt something."

"I think she did. She simply chose to discount it. Joining the Church is a huge change for people. It's not just a Sunday religion. It's a whole way of life. I think she knows it's true, but she isn't willing to live it."

"So she just pretended she'd never received a witness?"

"It's all about agency." Her companion shrugged. "The Spirit can only do so much, and then it's up to them. Believe it or not, this happens a lot."

"I hate it," Amanda said. "It seems so unfair."

"I know. And I have to say that I never get used to losing an investigator. Especially when I've gotten so close to them."

What if Kirsten and Chad were the ones from my dream and I couldn't help them after all? Amanda thought.

A cold wind blew past, scattering old leaves and newspapers along the street. Amanda pulled her jacket closer around her. She could keep the chill away from the outside, but the icy pain of her heartbreak inside wouldn't go away so easily.

Chapter Six

AMANDA LOOKED AT THE PILE of luggage sitting by the door. She'd been up early packing her things. Now she paced the floor, waiting for the APs to bring Sister Ferrari's new companion and take Amanda to her next area.

The sisters had been together four months, and though the transfer wasn't unexpected it still felt like a rude shock to Amanda. She knew it wasn't logical, but she resented the change. And she worried about adapting to a new area and companion.

"Sister Schultz should be a good companion for you," Sister Ferrari said. "I don't know her myself, but I heard she's due to go home fairly soon. That means she's bound to have lots of experience, and hopefully she won't be too trunky."

Amanda nodded but her mind was elsewhere. It felt like she was walking out in the middle of a movie without staying for the end.

"I hate this," Amanda said, turning toward the other sister. "I really care about the people here. How will I ever find out what happens to them?"

Sister Ferrari patted her companion's shoulder. "It's hard, but this is what it's all about. We serve in an area for a few weeks or a few months, and we grow to love the people. Then—bang—we're moved on, and someone else takes our place."

"Just because it happens all the time doesn't mean I have to like it." Amanda frowned.

"Of course you don't," Sister Ferrari agreed. "But I've always found it comforting to know that the work has been going on for years before I got here and will go on for years after I've gone. We're just small pieces in a huge tapestry."

She's probably right, Amanda thought. *But it doesn't make me feel any better.*

"Besides," Sister Ferrari winked, "isn't it nice to know that you were once a member of the famous district that beat the previous San Jose mission Book of Mormon record?"

Amanda couldn't help but laugh.

* * *

Elder Criddle and Elder Van were the APs who'd been sent to deliver Amanda and Sister Schultz to their new apartment. The midmorning traffic was light, and they were traveling at a good pace.

"I should probably warn you that this apartment has never had sisters in it," Criddle said. "The last elders were told to clean it up, but I wouldn't count on it."

The minivan pulled into the parking lot of a poorly kept apartment complex. Garbage blew around the blacktop, and the building looked desperately in need of a paint job.

"You have GOT to be kidding," Amanda's new companion said.

Sister Schultz was tall—over five foot ten—big boned, and muscular. Her short, thick, frizzy hair burst like a dark bush around her head, and she wore black-framed glasses.

Amanda collected her belongings, just two suitcases and a backpack. Sister Schultz had more than triple that amount. She'd brought four cardboard boxes so full they looked ready to explode, several clear plastic bins, two huge duffel bags, and a number of assorted-size suitcases.

The four missionaries, loaded down with luggage, began making their way to the second-floor apartment. It wasn't difficult to find since the previous occupants had taped a picture of Christ on the front door.

That's nice, thought Amanda. *Maybe the apartment won't be too bad after all.*

Elder Criddle shifted the luggage so he could use his right hand to stick the key into the lock and turn it. The second the door opened, a distinctive smell wafted toward them—a stale combination of dirty gym socks, sour milk, and cheap aftershave.

"You have GOT to be kidding!" Sister Schultz said again.

Elder Van hurried in and started opening windows throughout the apartment. "It just needs a little airing out."

Amanda cautiously stepped through the doorway and looked around. The living-room carpet was so badly stained and worn it was impossible to tell its original color. The walls were dirty and in need of new paint. She could see a hole in the Sheetrock behind the front door where the knob had broken through.

The kitchen proved even worse. The appliances were filthy, covered with a layer of greasy grime. Amanda's feet stuck to the linoleum, and she didn't dare get near the refrigerator. Turning around quickly, she headed toward the bedroom.

"You know what?" called Elder Van from the bathroom. "If I were you, I'd just spray everything in here with Lysol and bleach. Then leave it to soak overnight."

"No!" Sister Schultz said, her hands on her hips. "We are NOT staying here! Look at this place. It's horrible and it reeks," she said, throwing open the fridge door. "And look at all the moldy food. This place is not habitable. It should be condemned."

"Now, Sister," Elder Criddle said. "It's nothing that a little bit of elbow grease won't solve. Just give the ward Relief Society a call. I'm sure they would be happy to help you get this place into shape."

As he talked, he slowly backed toward the front door, motioning discreetly for his companion to join him.

"Yeah," added Elder Van. "That's what they're for. Relief."

"You can't just leave us here!" Sister Schultz insisted. "There's got to be somewhere else we can stay."

"Sister Schultz, trust me. This is it. I'm really sorry, but there isn't anything else we can do."

Elder Criddle tossed a key ring at Amanda, and instinctively she raised her hand and caught it. A fraction of a second later, he and his companion were out the door and down the stairs.

"Elder Criddle! You get back here!" yelled Sister Schultz, following them out. "Elders!"

But neither of them turned around. "We'll call you tomorrow and see how it's going," called Elder Criddle over his shoulder as he climbed into the minivan. "Good luck! Oh, and the green Corolla in the parking lot is yours! Now go do some good!"

"I'm going to do some good to your face the next time I see you!" she yelled after them. "Do you hear me?" But they were already in the van.

Amanda watched her companion in amazement. Sister Schultz kicked at the stairs in frustration and then stomped back in. She prepared to slam the apartment door, but apparently thought better of it as she caught a whiff of the air. She choked and shook her head in disgust. "The nerve!"

"Maybe we ought to look for some cleaning supplies," Amanda suggested in a hesitant voice.

Sister Schultz glanced at her companion quickly. "Do you still have those keys?" she asked.

Amanda nodded.

"Give them to me, comp," she said, holding out her hand. "We definitely need to clean, but I'm not touching a thing in here until I have a pair of rubber gloves on my hands. I saw a store back on the main road a few miles. Let's go stock up on garbage bags and disinfectant."

At least we're doing something positive about the apartment, Amanda thought as she followed her companion down the stairs.

"What do you want to bet the car is out of gas?" predicted Sister Schultz.

She was right, and they had to drive on fumes for three blocks to a gas station.

Once they reached the store, Sister Schultz began filling her cart. She picked up most of the cleaning supplies the store carried, and the basket was quickly filled with plastic garbage bags, cleaning solutions, rubber gloves, a broom, mop, pail, and a dozen assorted sponges.

From a colorful Christmas baking display Sister Schultz continued loading up on a variety of cooking supplies—white and brown sugar, flour, spices, nuts, and a huge bag of chocolate chips.

"Uh, Sister Schultz?" Amanda said. "This is an awful lot of stuff, and I don't have much money left this month. Perhaps we should—"

"One word, comp. *Credit.* One of the benefits of being a little older 'than the average missionary,'" she said in a Yogi Bear voice, "is that one brings along a few luxuries, such as my darling MC." She produced a MasterCard from her wallet and kissed it.

"But I still don't have enough money for my half," continued Amanda in dismay.

"I told you, don't worry," Sister Schultz said again. "My dad told me to use this for the essentials, and he makes the payments while I'm out here. It's a system that's worked great for the past sixteen and a half months."

Amanda was uncomfortable with the arrangement, but she didn't know what else she could do. She followed along as the contents in her companion's cart seemed to grow exponentially. When they finally reached the checkout counter and the items were added up, Amanda was shocked to find the amount totaled $272. "You really think your dad will pay that?" Amanda asked in amazement.

"Oh, he's paid more, and if he asks, I'll just explain about everything, and he'll understand immediately. He's just so happy to have me out on a mission that he makes sure I have everything I need."

Back at the apartment, they unloaded the groceries onto the outside walkway. They agreed not to risk bringing food into the apartment until they had disinfected a few surfaces. After changing clothes, they began scrubbing the kitchen. Amanda took the refrigerator while Sister Schultz washed the walls and counters.

An hour into their cleaning a female voice called out from the doorway. "Yoo-hoo! Anybody home?"

Amanda began to get up, but Sister Schultz was already yelling, "It's open! Come on in! We're back here!"

Shrugging her shoulders, Amanda turned around and waited for their visitor to make her way into the kitchen.

"Oh, Sisters, this is awful," the woman said as she looked around in disgust. "I knew it was going to be messy, but I had no idea it had gotten this bad."

"Elders!" Sister Schultz said by way of explanation.

The woman laughed in response. "That's true, I guess. I'm Brenda Taylor, a member of the ward, and I live downstairs."

Brenda was in her mid-thirties and wore a bright orange muumuu that covered her squat, pear-shaped figure. Amanda got up and shook her hand. "I'm Sister Kelly, and this is my companion, Sister Schultz."

Sister Schultz waved briefly. She was furiously scrubbing the wall—so hard that some of the paint came off.

"Listen, let me change my clothes and come back and help. We live one floor down, and my kids are in school until three, so I have about four hours free."

"That would be so nice," Amanda said gratefully.

"I won't be a minute," Brenda said as she hurried out the door.

"That's more like it," Sister Schultz said over her shoulder. "Everything always goes better when the ward members get involved."

Brenda took a little longer than a minute—nearly thirty, to be exact. But when she returned, she was loaded down with cleaning supplies and had another woman with her.

"This is Kay," Brenda said, motioning toward a tall angular woman in her mid-fifties. "Kay is in the Relief Society presidency."

Amanda smiled. It amused her the way Church members often introduced each other with their callings, as if they were official titles of some sort. *Bob Jones, attorney-at-law, meet Bill Smith, CTR 5 teacher.*

"Kay's husband is going to drop by tonight after work and take a look at this place. He's in the Young Men presidency, and he thinks he can get some of the priesthood together to paint and recarpet," finished Brenda.

Amanda was touched. "How can we thank you?"

"We women need to stick together," Kay said, and they all laughed.

With the extra help, they finished quickly. By the time Brenda and Kay left, they had the kitchen and bathroom scrubbed, the food put away, and four huge black garbage bags sitting by the door ready to be taken out.

They'd found a number of "treasures" in their cleaning: several neckties in a variety of ugly patterns stuffed under a bed, a pile of *Ensign* magazines that had been used to prop up one corner of the sofa, and a desk drawer containing photos of a pretty blond girl—including her wedding announcement.

However, the most interesting find was a large picture on the floor at the back of the closet. It was a print of Jesus—His arms outstretched, inviting all to come to Him. The picture itself was not unusual, but when they turned it over they found at least fifty different elders' signatures—probably all past occupants of the apartment. Brenda had known some of them. Elder Fullmer, Elder Hernandez, Elder Keller, and Elder Stapleton were fairly recent additions. But some of the earlier ones were faded and worn. Still, they could make out most of the names—Elder Nelson, Elder VanOstendorff, Elder Zelaya, and others. It was anyone's guess how long they'd been there.

"It appears that you sisters are the first females in this place—at least according to this unofficial history," Kay said. "Why don't you add your names?"

"Good idea," Sister Schultz said as she wrote hers in large, flamboyant strokes.

When it was Amanda's turn, she signed in small, careful script below her companion's. They hung the picture on the newly cleaned living room wall.

Well, we've got the apartment clean, thought Amanda, adjusting the frame so that it hung straight. *I wonder what's next.*

* * *

Sister Schultz proved to be an excellent cook if the dinner she made that night was any indication. Once they finished eating, the next project was to try and make sense of the area book that had been left by the last set of missionaries.

"This thing is a mess," Sister Schultz said in disgust. "I can't make heads or tails of it. We should probably just toss it and start over."

Amanda grabbed the book protectively. This might be their only source of information on the history of the work in this ward.

"Why don't you let me have a try first?" she asked.

"Sure, go for it," Sister Schultz said, getting up. "I need to give my mom a call and let her know I've been transferred."

"You're calling home?" asked Amanda in surprise. "Did you get permission?"

"Well . . . not exactly. The thing is . . . the rule was set up to keep missionaries from getting sidetracked, and for some missionaries that might be a problem. But not for me."

"But won't they know you called when they see the phone bill?"

Sister Schultz smiled. "See, now that's just the kind of thing I thought when I was new," she said. "But if I use a calling card, it doesn't show up on the bill."

Amanda tried again. "Why don't you just write her a note? Or if you wait till P-day you could send her an e-mail from the library."

But Sister Schultz only laughed. "I can see you're quite the little rule keeper. Don't worry. It will only take a minute."

Amanda didn't know what to say. She watched uncomfortably as her companion dialed the number and waited until someone picked up on the other end.

"Hi, Mom," she said, making herself comfortable on the floor by the phone. "So, how are things going today?"

Feeling troubled, Amanda turned her attention back to the area book. It obviously hadn't been updated for several weeks. Many of the names and scribbled notes along the margins were hard to read. She took out a pen and a sheet of clean paper and began translating. It wasn't long until the challenge of her project replaced the irritation she felt toward her companion.

I could sure use a Urim and Thummim about now.

Thirty minutes passed, and Sister Schultz was still on the phone chatting with her mother. In the meantime, Amanda had come up with a list of five names with addresses and phone numbers. She couldn't tell their ages or whether they were single or married, and in some cases she wasn't even sure if they were male or female.

"You take care, Mom. I love you too . . . I know. Only a few more weeks. I can't wait! Bye." Sister Schultz hung up the receiver and wandered over to the table to look over Amanda's shoulder. "Did you find all those names from that disaster of an area book?" she asked in amazement.

"It took a bit of work," Amanda answered, "but at least we have somewhere to start."

Sister Schultz kicked off her shoes. "Let's stop by Sister Taylor's apartment on our way out tomorrow and get a ward list. By the way, did they tell you why they kicked the last elders out of this area?"

Amanda shook her head. "Were they kicked out? I was told they were transferred out together."

"That's missionary speak for 'kicked out.' They must have been really screwing around to pull them both out and put in sisters."

Amanda wasn't sure how to respond.

Just then, the phone rang and Sister Schultz hurried over to answer it. "Hello? Oh, hi, Elder Hoff, this is Sister Schultz."

She looked over at Amanda and rolled her eyes. "We got in okay, no thanks to those stinkin' OFFICE elders. The place was a pigsty."

Amanda continued to be amazed at the outspoken nature of her companion—so different from her own.

"Yeah, well . . . it's always nice to offer after the job is already done." She listened for a few moments, then grimaced at Amanda and rolled her eyes again. "You kept getting voice mail? I don't know, maybe the phone was off the hook or something," she said sweetly. "Sure, we could meet you tomorrow for lunch. Where and when? . . . Okay, we'll be there . . . 'Night."

"DLs," she said, hanging up the phone. "They are the worst. Hey, do you want some ice cream?"

"No, I'm fine," Amanda answered. "So, do you know the district leader?"

"Hoff? Oh, yeah. He was a junior companion in one of my areas. Not one of my favorite elders," she said.

I'm beginning to notice a pattern, Amanda thought. "Who is your favorite elder?"

"Hmm. Gotta say Elder Jeffrey R. Holland."

"You mean the Apostle?"

"Yeah, that's the one. Now there is an elder I can trust and respect," Sister Schultz said with conviction.

"I meant here in the mission," pressed Amanda.

"In or out of the mission, it's Elder Holland."

"I know they're kind of young, but all the elders I've met really seem to be trying to do what's right," Amanda said.

"Yeah, well, comp, you haven't been out all that long, have you?"

Feeling a little slighted, Amanda decided to drop the subject.

Sister Schultz went into the kitchen, and Amanda could hear the freezer door opening.

Maybe she's one of those people who seem arrogant until you get to know them. I guess I just need to get to know her better.

Sister Schultz returned a few minutes later with a huge bowl of ice cream.

"So," Amanda began. "You said you were from Montana, right?"

"Yup, a little northeast of Great Falls. My parents have a cattle ranch up there. It's got to be the most beautiful place on earth."

This was more like it. "Do you have any brothers and sisters?" she asked.

"Just brothers. Two older and three younger."

Amanda could imagine Sister Schultz in a family of active boys. "Are they into sports?"

"Nah, not unless you call rolling around in the dirt and beating each other senseless a sport," she said. "The one below me is on a mission now too. Argentina."

"So you're both out together," Amanda said. "That's really nice."

"I guess. Actually, the mission will be good for him. Always was kind of a cocky kid." Sister Schultz finished her ice cream. "So, tomorrow I guess we can start working on that list of yours. But right now I'm exhausted," Sister Schultz said, yawning widely and heading for bed.

As she disappeared into the bedroom, Amanda felt a great longing for her last companion. Amanda could already tell that working with this sister would be nothing like her experiences before. As she locked the doors and windows and checked to make sure the lights were off before heading to bed, a feeling of resentment began to grow inside her. She tried to ignore it by saying her prayers and reading her scriptures, but she could still feel it gnawing at her like a low-grade headache.

To distract herself, she thought about Jake, but that was a mistake. A familiar longing overwhelmed her, and she wished she could just pick up the phone and call him. It would be so good to hear his voice. Perhaps it would dispel the vague uneasiness she'd begun to sense about him over the last few weeks—something she felt but couldn't put her finger on. But of course she couldn't call him. Just because her companion didn't seem to want to obey the rules was no reason for her to do the same.

Getting into bed, Amanda's mind moved to her dream and the family she was looking for. They'd had a few baptisms in their last area, but Amanda was sure she hadn't found the family she was looking for.

Glancing at Sister Schultz asleep and snoring loudly in the other bed, Amanda sighed. Would her companion help or hinder her as Amanda searched for the family she was seeking to unite?

Chapter Seven

December 14, 2008

Dear Jake,

Just a quick note to let you know that I have been transferred. I'm serving in Santa Clara, right in the heart of the mission.

My new companion is an interesting person—very casual about everything from her appearance to her work standard. I think she may be a challenge to work with, but I'm sure I can find a way to get through to her.

Is everything okay with you? Classes going all right? You just seem a bit distracted in your letters. You know I love you, and if there is anything I can do to help, or if you just want to talk. Well, you know I'm here. I really miss you!

Love always,
Amanda

THE NEXT MORNING, AMANDA GOT up at six-thirty as usual and took a shower. When she got out, Sister Schultz was just beginning to drag herself out of bed. By the time Sister Schultz finally came to the table for companionship study it was eight forty-five, fifteen minutes before they had to leave.

"So, how do you want to do this?" Amanda asked. "We can pick up where Sister Ferrari and I left off if you want."

Sister Schultz settled back in her chair. "Actually, I really get a lot more out of personal study than companion study, and I image it's the same for you. So why don't we just dispense with the companion study thing and use the extra time for our own stuff, okay?"

She wasn't really asking for Amanda's approval, and she didn't wait for a response. Instead, she opened her journal and turned all her attention to writing while Amanda just sat there staring in amazement.

"I really think we should follow the mission rules on this," Amanda said. "We can study whatever you want, but don't you think we should do it together?"

Sister Schultz glared up at her. "Look, you can do what you want, but I've already told you. I don't do companion study."

There was nothing else for Amanda to do but continue her own studies in silence.

Once they left the apartment, the sisters spent the rest of the morning in the car getting lost as they searched for the addresses on Amanda's list. Sister Schultz, who insisted on driving, had a horrible sense of direction.

"Turn left," Amanda said as they approached an intersection. Sister Schultz put on her right blinker and moved into the right lane. "Not that left. The other left."

"Well, why didn't you say so?" she said as she jerked into traffic, barely making the left turn and causing several cars to slam on their brakes. "I just hate California drivers, don't you? They really don't know what they're doing."

Amanda forced herself to keep quiet.

At last they found the first address and met the young professional man who lived there. "I'm just running out the door to work," he said after the sisters introduced themselves. "You're welcome to come back if you like, but I don't think we're interested."

"Who's at the door?" called another male voice from within the house. A moment later a young African-American man came up behind the first and put his hand affectionately on the other's shoulder.

"They're sister missionaries from the Mormon Church. I told them we weren't really interested."

"That's true," agreed the second. "But thank you for coming by."

As they walked back to the car, Sister Schultz leaned over and whispered to her companion, "I don't think they're ready for the proclamation on the family, do you?"

Amanda had to smile. "Probably not."

The second stop was an apartment building in a run-down part of town. Amanda passed a vacant lot full of weeds and litter that sided up against the building. Several young children were playing there and looked up when the sisters passed. Their clothes were worn and dirty, and Amanda was surprised by how hardened their faces seemed when compared to their young bodies.

Once inside, a little girl with dirty, tangled hair answered their knocks. From the door the room looked filthy and smelled of musty marijuana. "Mommy's sleeping right now, and she'll be mad if I wake her up," the child said.

"Don't worry," Amanda assured her. "We can come back later." But as she walked out with her companion, Amanda felt heartsick. *How can Heavenly Father send any of His beautiful spirit children down to places like this?* She shook her head. *That poor child probably had everything against her from the moment she was born. It isn't fair.*

By lunchtime, they'd located all five of the houses on the list. One family no longer lived at the address, and the present occupants didn't know how to reach them. Another was an older man who made it clear that missionaries were not welcome in his home and that if they showed up again he would call the police. The last turned out to be a writer who'd been interviewing the elders as part of his research for a new book but had since changed his mind, deciding that the life of a missionary was too boring.

"It's like we're walking through the great and spacious building in Lehi's dream, trying to offer people a bite of the fruit and they're so wrapped up in their own sins and pride that they can't see how unhappy they are," Amanda said.

"My trainer told me once that there is so much pain and suffering in this world that we can't possibly fix it all. No one can," Sister Schultz said. "But if people would just accept the gospel and live it, the Lord could heal them, and then they could fix their own lives."

Amanda looked at her companion, surprised. Perhaps there was more to Sister Schultz than met the eye.

They pulled up in front of a diner called Wimpy's Burgers and found the elders already there, waiting in a booth toward the back. As the sisters approached, both elders stood.

"Hi, Sister Schultz. And you must be Sister Kelly. I'm Elder Hoff, and this is my companion, Elder Lee." He motioned toward the young man at his left. Hoff was short and slender with close-set gray eyes and missionary-cut blond hair that he wore spiked with gel. He reminded Amanda of Bart Simpson. His companion was Asian with dark eyes and a contagious smile. He was smiling now.

"Hi," he said. "Nice to have some sisters in the district."

Amanda found herself smiling back. There was an open friendliness about him that was engaging. *I wonder if their investigators feel this when he teaches.*

A young waitress with short dark hair and brown eyes walked up to the table and handed the missionaries their menus.

"What can I get you?" she asked with a slight Hispanic accent, looking around the table.

"A number six and a root beer for me, Maria," Elder Hoff said, "and the same for him."

Maria grinned as she jotted down their orders on a notepad. "Ladies?"

"Are the chocolate milkshakes good here?" Sister Schultz asked.

"I guess so."

"I'll take a large then, and a number five with extra bacon."

"Just water and a small chef salad for me, thank you," Amanda said as she unfolded a paper napkin and placed it on her lap.

Once the waitress left, Elder Hoff turned his attention to Sister Schultz. "So, has the morning been productive?"

"Ask my comp, the boss," she said, motioning with her head toward Amanda. Elder Hoff raised his eyebrows slightly and turned his attention to her.

Amanda shifted in her seat, uncomfortable at being forced to take the lead. "We came up with a list of names from the area book. It wasn't very up-to-date, though."

"That doesn't surprise me," Elder Hoff interrupted. "Somehow I don't think that the last set of elders had record keeping as a high priority."

"That's an understatement," Sister Schultz said. "Apparently cleaning wasn't on the list at all. So what exactly did the elders do? All that the president said was that there were problems."

The elders exchanged knowing glances, and Elder Hoff said, "We can't really tell you . . . because it's confidential. But let's just say that if there was a mission rule they didn't break, I don't know about it."

"I hate missionaries who think that the rules apply to everyone but themselves," Schultz said.

Amanda glanced at her companion, but the girl didn't seem to see the hypocrisy in her statement.

Elder Hoff changed the subject. "We have district meetings every Tuesday at the Quince Street building. Ten AM sharp. So if you need more pass-along cards or copies of the Book of Mormon or anything, let me know and I'll bring them to the meeting."

"I'm not sure we have any at the apartment," Amanda said, thinking back to their house cleaning the day before.

"I thought that might be the case. I have some in the car, so don't leave without getting them. Oh, and zone conference will be coming up in a few weeks."

"Will we be doing priesthood interviews with the president?" Amanda asked.

"I think so. The zone leaders did the interviews last time, right Lee?"

Elder Lee nodded in agreement.

"And one more thing," Elder Hoff said. "We are having a district activity next week, and . . ."

"Let me guess," Sister Schultz said. "You're playing basketball, and you want the sisters to cook, like always."

Elder Hoff grinned. "Well, it's actually volleyball, but yeah, if you guys would do the lunch . . ."

The conversation stopped as Maria returned with their lunches and the four missionaries concentrated on eating.

"How do you suggest we approach this area?" Amanda asked, wiping a bit of salad dressing off her lips with a paper napkin.

Hoff's mouth was too full of fries to answer, so Elder Lee responded instead. "I'm afraid you're going to have to spend some time on damage control. The previous elders screwed around a lot. They blew off appointments and irritated a lot of the members. It's going to take a while to rebuild the trust in the ward."

"Do you have a ward list?" Hoff asked.

Amanda pulled it out of her purse. "We have it right here."

"Good, then you can go out and introduce yourself to the Relief Society president. Maybe get an idea of who the part-member families are."

"Already done," Sister Schultz said with a grin. "We have a dinner appointment with her family tonight."

Elder Hoff smiled. "Right on the ball. You two won't have any trouble, I can tell."

Amanda hoped he was right.

After lunch they headed back to the car. "So, where to now?" Sister Schultz asked.

Amanda considered her question. None of the names in the area book had paid off, and she was anxious to get back to her search for the family from her dream. "Maybe we could do some tracting?"

"No," Schultz said. "I don't tract. Tracting is the least successful method there is of proselyting."

"That may be true," Amanda agreed. "But right now we don't have a single investigator. What do you suggest we do?"

"I have an idea," Sister Schultz said, winking and clucking her tongue. "It's sharing the gospel, but it's a lot more fun than tracting."

Sister Schultz drove around the area until they found a large grocery store with a parking lot full of cars. They pulled in at the far end and got out.

"We're going grocery shopping?" Amanda asked.

"No, we're planting seeds," Sister Schultz responded, handing her a small stack of *Lamb of God* video pass-along cards.

"What you do is find someone with a cart full of groceries or with a bunch of small children and help them unload the bags into their car. When they thank you, or if they try to tip you, you refuse but hand them one of these cards and wish them a nice day. It's fun. People are always so shocked."

"I'll bet," Amanda said. The last thing she wanted to do was interrupt strangers while they were shopping. Besides, her trainer had never done anything like this. It probably wasn't really breaking the rules, but Amanda wondered how effective it would be at getting them new investigators.

"Watch," Schultz said, walking over to a young mother standing next to a minivan. A cart nearly overflowing with grocery bags stood waiting by the open door while the woman struggled to buckle her wiggly toddler into a car seat. Sister Schultz began loading the bags into the back of the van. The woman was startled at first, but once she realized that Sister Schultz meant her no harm, she seemed grateful and took the card with a smile.

Well, I guess it's worth a try. Amanda looked around and saw an elderly lady struggling to carry several plastic bags.

"Here, let me help you with those," Amanda said.

The woman eyed her suspiciously.

"Really, it's okay," Amanda assured her. "I just want to help."

After looking her over carefully, the woman smiled and handed Amanda a couple of the heavier bags. Once everything was safely stowed in the trunk, the old lady thanked Amanda and accepted the card.

She probably won't call, Amanda thought as she watched the car pull out of the parking lot. *But I have to admit that it feels nice to be helping others.*

The hour passed quickly, and together the sister missionaries gave away fifteen cards.

"Wasn't that a lot better than tracting?" Sister Schultz asked, climbing back into the car. She was eating a candy bar that an elderly man had pressed on her.

"Well, it was fun," Amanda admitted, "but I still don't see how it helps us find people to teach."

"Someone plants the seeds, and someone else fertilizes and waters, and then someone else will pick the fruit. It doesn't matter who does what, right?" Sister Schultz shrugged her shoulders.

"I . . . I guess," Amanda said hesitantly.

"So today we planted. Who knows where the seeds will land or how they'll grow. But at least the seeds are out there."

"But, as missionaries, aren't we supposed to be harvesting?" Amanda asked.

"Missionary work is missionary work." Sister Schultz started the car. "I have a dozen creative methods for sharing the gospel. We shouldn't ever have to tract."

Amanda felt a wave of depression settle over her.

* * *

December 23, 2008

Dear Amanda,

Sorry it's taken me so long to write, and I hope this care package reaches you before Christmas. I've been so busy with school and then trying to get home for the holidays. Looks like I'll be making honor roll this semester. Not bad for a boy who's been out of school for over two years, huh?

So what will you be doing for Christmas? I got invited by one of the girls in my stake to go to the New Years Eve dance. I know we didn't talk about dating before you left, but she's just a friend and I figured you wouldn't mind. Keep up the good work.

Love,
Jake

The next two weeks seemed to drag by, and they still hadn't found any investigators.

Christmas came and Amanda got to call her family. It was good to hear their voices, but it made her feel homesick. She asked them about Jake, but her mother said he hadn't been over to visit since the end of September.

Despite her best efforts, the ward members, though pleasant enough, continued to be unsupportive. She and her companion had only received two dinner invitations since arriving—one from the Relief Society president when they first arrived and the second from the bishop and his family on New Year's Day.

Bishop Fife was an attractive man in his mid-thirties. He and his wife, Anna, lived in an expensive and beautifully decorated home. Sister Fife had exquisite taste in clothing, and Amanda admired the woman's outfit, a jade blue suit with a touch of white silk at the neck. It was exactly the type of clothing that Amanda herself chose, although without the pricey designer names attached.

Dinner was served on fine china, with goblets and cloth napkins.

"You guys went all out," Sister Schultz said, sitting down at the table. "You even have all the extra forks and spoons and stuff."

"We wanted to invite you over earlier," Sister Fife said. "But my husband travels so much for his job, and then most weekends are taken up with his Church responsibilities."

"That must be tough," Amanda said.

Sister Fife glanced at her two daughters, one eight and the other ten, who sat across from the sisters. Neither child had said a word all through the meal. "It's especially hard for them."

Turning back toward the bishop, Amanda cleared her throat. "I wonder if you've given any more thought to our idea to push a ward missionary referral program?"

Bishop Fife removed his napkin from his lap and dropped it by the side of his plate. "Oh, it's an excellent idea and I'm all for it. I just am not sure with the holidays and all if this is the best time to start. Our ward mission leader and his wife are still in Fiji, and I'm going to be traveling for the next two weeks. Perhaps we could talk about doing something in late January."

"I hate to push it off so far . . ." Amanda began.

Bishop Fife leaned forward. "The thing is that we have a very busy ward. It's not like I don't want to go forward with this, but I think that home teaching, temple attendance, and keeping the youth out of trouble are higher priorities right now."

Sister Schultz dropped her knife on the edge of the plate with a sharp ringing noise. "I need to be honest with you. I think your ward needs to do more to reach out to the less-active members," she said.

Amanda tried to nudge her companion under the table. They'd discussed this issue in the car on the way over, and Amanda thought she'd convinced Sister Schultz to wait until their Sunday meetings to bring it up.

Bishop Fife raised his eyebrows. "Really?"

"Several people say they don't feel comfortable at church because they don't have a lot of money. They say that they feel looked down on and unaccepted because their cars are old and they don't have the money to buy expensive church clothes."

"Well, that is ridiculous," Sister Fife said. "We are a very friendly and generous ward. People who won't make the effort to participate in church are always looking for someone else to blame it on."

"You don't think a big house and fancy clothes might be intimidating to people who are poorer than you?" Sister Schultz asked.

Amanda jumped in. "I think what my companion means to say is that those of us who are active need to make sure we reach out and include those who don't come out much."

The atmosphere in the room had cooled considerably, and it was with great relief that the sisters were able to leave the home a short time later.

That night, Amanda sat in the living room feeling alone and discouraged. She and Sister Schultz had argued in the car all the way home. Now her companion was in their room, presumably reading her scriptures while Amanda was in the living room waiting for the DL's nightly check-in call and trying to study.

Amanda set her scriptures on the couch and pulled out a snapshot of her and Jake at Utah Lake. He'd given it to her just before he'd left on his mission, and Amanda had always kept it in her quad. On the back he'd written, "To the love of my life, Jake." As she flipped it over and studied his face, Amanda suddenly felt a great longing for Jake's company, the feel of his arms around her, and the sound of his voice. He would know what to say to make her feel better. At least, he had before her mission. Now she wasn't so sure.

Lately his letters weren't coming as often as they had when she'd first come out, and the few he did send were short and, in an indefinable way, less personal. She'd tried to ignore the nagging doubts for several weeks now, but tonight, with her defenses low, she couldn't help but worry. And then there was the dream. The pressure to find the people from the picture seemed even stronger tonight, making her lack of control over the situation even more frustrating.

What was she going to do?

Chapter Eight

December 26, 2008

Dear Jake,

Thank you for the Christmas package. It was thoughtful of your mom to include some of her fudge. The gloves and scarf were nice too. We don't have snow here, but sometimes in the evenings the temperature gets down into the forties so I'm sure I'll be able to use them.

This area I'm in is so diverse—a huge melting pot of ages, nationalities, and financial status. We have a Laotian woman who lives in the apartment to our right, and a family from Honduras on our left. There are several gated communities with huge, expensive homes, and most of our active ward members are quite affluent.

You asked in your last letter how we spent Christmas. The mission president had a special dinner at his house, and my companion and I made cookies and delivered them to the less-active members of the ward. It wasn't home, but it was nice.

I think it's great that you're going to the New Year's Eve dance. I went out on a few dates myself while you were on your mission. I don't expect you to be a monk or anything while I'm gone. But just remember how much I love you and miss you. Next Christmas we will be together! I can hardly wait.

Love you forever,
Amanda

THE NEXT MORNING AT BREAKFAST, Amanda brought in the missionary rule book, known affectionately to the missionaries as the "little white bible." She'd been reading through it so she could point out to Sister Schultz the place where it stated that companions were supposed to study together each day.

"It's a rule," Amanda said. "Even if we don't agree with it, we should still follow it, just for obedience's sake."

Sister Schultz finished the last bite of her cereal, rinsed out the bowl, and sat back down at the table before responding. "The thing you don't understand, Sister Kelly, is how rules work. You don't actually have to follow them to be obedient."

Amanda leaned back in her chair.

"What do the scriptures say is one of the most important rules that we have in the Church?"

"Love the Lord thy God," Amanda said.

"Granted, that one is important, too," Sister Schultz waved her hand as if brushing away a mosquito. "But I was thinking of the Word of Wisdom, which is basically a set of health rules, right?"

Amanda spread her hands apart. "I guess."

"At the end there's a verse that says how the rule was written so clearly that even the weakest, most brain-dead member of the Church would be able to understand it."

Amanda had never heard the Word of Wisdom described in quite that way before, but her companion didn't wait for her response before moving on.

"This is a perfect example of the letter of the law. As the scripture explained, the letter of the law is given for people who are not very bright, so that they have no room to say, 'I didn't get it. I was confused.'"

"I don't think that really applies to this situation . . ." Amanda began, but her companion continued on.

"Now, the spirit of the law is higher. It looks at the letter of the law and says, 'What was the point of this rule, and what is it supposed to accomplish?' Once you figure that out, then as long as you achieve that end, the means you use no longer really matter. You're following the spirit of the law."

Amanda listened carefully while trying to prepare an argument to her companion's obviously flawed reasoning. But before she could say anything,

Sister Schultz got up, walked out of the kitchen, and went into the bathroom.

* * *

Later that day Amanda and her companion walked down the street to visit a ward member. They were running low on gas, and Amanda had insisted they walk.

A pale sun struggled to shine through the hazy sky, but the temperature was in the sixties and a few hardy pansies lent a touch of color to the otherwise drab sidewalk.

Their teaching pool was still empty, and Amanda tried again to talk her companion into tracting, but Sister Schultz stubbornly refused.

"I told you before. I don't tract."

"But we're running out of options," Amanda said. "We can't get the members to refer people, and the part-member families haven't shown any interest. I don't think we have any other options."

"Whenever I've tried to tract, I've had only bad experiences. Besides, people don't want to be bothered with strangers knocking at their doors. That's why I try to approach when they're more receptive to conversation with strangers."

"For example?" Amanda asked.

"Like when they're sitting at a bus stop or standing in line to buy food."

Amanda shook her head. "We don't take the bus, and we can't hang out at grocery stores all day."

"Well, it beats wearing out your knuckles banging on doors where no one wants you."

Amanda gave up, shaking her head in frustration, hardly noticing the large building they passed. It was in the process of being remodeled. A complicated maze of scaffolding had been erected across the front. At least a dozen construction workers filled the area. Some were perched high up on the walls tearing off old masonry while others were busy unloading sheet rock from the bed of a truck into a tall pile by the front door.

Amanda turned to her companion, prepared to resume her argument about tracting, when a loud wolf whistle caught her attention. She looked back at the building and noticed that several of the men had stopped working to watch them walk past. A few yelled out vulgar comments about the sisters' bodies, and one particularly loud-mouthed worker with a scraggily beard and a beer belly suggested they meet him after work so he could show them a "good time." More rude laughter and whistles followed.

Amanda was both embarrassed and outraged. She could feel her face turning red, and she picked up the pace, not running, but certainly going faster until she was out of earshot.

"What animals!" Amanda said a half block later. "I'd like to slap every one of them. It's not like I've never heard that kind of garbage before. But don't they have any respect? We are missionaries for Pete's sake."

"How would they know?" answered Sister Schultz. "You flew out of there too fast for anyone to even get a glimpse of your name tag."

Amanda stared at her in surprise. "What are you talking about?"

"I'm just saying that there might have been a teaching opportunity there. I mean we did have their attention, right?" Sister Schultz popped a stick of gum into her mouth and began chewing.

"Are you crazy? It was pretty evident where they directed their attention."

Sister Schultz laughed. "They didn't know what else we had to offer, did they?"

Amanda shook her head. "Even if we'd tried talking to them about the Church, they would have just harassed us more."

"You think so?" Sister Schultz looked thoughtful. "I say we give it a try and see."

"What? You aren't really thinking of going back there, are you?"

Sister Schultz grinned. "They're still God's children, like you and me. By the way, do you have that stack of pass-along cards we picked up at the district meeting yesterday?"

"I really don't think—" began Amanda, but Sister Schultz had already turned around.

Amanda considered standing there and letting her companion jump off the cliff by herself. But that would be breaking the rules, and Amanda couldn't do that. She hurried to catch up despite the mental image of a bunch of smelly men trying to overpower her as she desperately swung her backpack full of copies of the Book of Mormon at them.

As they approached the construction site, Amanda hung back. It wasn't long before the men became aware of their presence, eyeing them curiously. From somewhere above, a male voice shouted, "Hey baby, you want a piece of me?" and several others laughed, but the noise stopped abruptly as Sister Schultz stepped forward to face the group.

"Gentlemen, we would like to take a moment to introduce ourselves. We're missionaries from The Church of Jesus Christ of Latter-day Saints." She spoke loudly and clearly. "We are dedicating a year and a half of our time, at our own expense, to preach the gospel of Jesus Christ to the people of the San Jose area. Since you have all expressed an interest in our presence in your community—"

Amanda did her best to suppress a nervous giggle. There was no doubt her companion had a unique sense of humor.

A tall man with broad shoulders and a florescent yellow hard hat strode out of the building and stood with his hands folded in front of him, but didn't interrupt the proceedings.

"We'd like each of you to take one of these cards. If you call the number on the back, they'll send you a free copy of the Book of Mormon."

She motioned for Amanda to pass out the cards. With trembling hands, she walked forward and handed each man a card. Most of the men wouldn't look at her, but the tall man near the building stared intently. His attention made her nervous, and Amanda moved away quickly.

Sister Schultz continued. "We come by here often, and we would be happy to answer any and all questions you might have about our Church."

The tall man stepped forward and sauntered toward them, pushing the hard hat back from his face. Amanda panicked. She grabbed Sister Schultz by the arm, and with all the energy she could muster, she dragged her down the sidewalk.

"Have a nice day, and we'll see you again soon!" yelled Sister Schultz over her shoulder before turning to her companion. "What did you pull me away for? He looked like he had a question!" Sister Schultz said.

"He looked like he was going to accost us," corrected Amanda.

"At any rate, did you see the looks on their faces? I guarantee you those men will never bother a sister missionary again." Schultz chuckled.

The whole encounter had gone better than she'd expected. Still, Amanda's heart was racing and she felt shaky. "We could have been attacked, or worse. What were you thinking?"

"No one was going to attack us on a main street," Sister Schultz pointed out. "That only happens in alleyways at night."

* * *

February 2, 2009

Dear Jake,

I haven't heard from you in over a month. Is everything okay? Maybe you did write and it got lost in the mail. I can't help worrying a little, though.

My companion is driving me nuts. I never knew it could be so hard to live and work with another person. I guess I was spoiled with my trainer. Oh, well. Write soon and let me know that everything is fine with you. I miss you more than I can say. Oh, and Happy Valentine's Day. You know I'm always yours!

Love,
Amanda

Zone conference was held at the stake center later that week, and Amanda was dreading her interview with President Edwards. He would ask about the work in their area and how she and Sister Schultz were getting along, and Amanda didn't know what she would say. If she told him everything was great, then she would be lying, but if she told him the truth, he might think she was trying to get her companion in trouble.

President Edwards had always reminded Amanda of her late grandpa Kelly. Though the president was much younger, probably in his early fifties, he had the same large build and the same look in his eyes—a combination of kindness and humor. Amanda had no doubt he could be firm when necessary, but usually his face bore a warm smile, and he had a way of inspiring confidence in others.

"I've been trying so hard," Amanda was saying as she sat across from him in the bishop's office he was using for interviews. "But I just don't know what to do. Sister Schultz is so stubborn and refuses to see any point of view but her own."

That look of amusement appeared in President Edward's eyes now, but he merely motioned with his hand, encouraging her to continue.

Amanda recounted the problems she'd had getting Sister Schultz to study with her, the phone calls home, and the weird finding methods she'd employed. "And she refuses to tract at all. The Lord won't bless us unless we obey the rules, but I just can't get her to cooperate."

When she finished, President Edwards rubbed the bridge of his nose and then cleared his throat. "I know you and Sister Schultz have been having your struggles, and it might be difficult for you to see, but your companion is a good missionary. She's had a lot of hard things happen to her out here, and I know she can be a little difficult sometimes, but she has a heart of gold and I think there is a lot you can learn from her."

Amanda couldn't think of anything Sister Schultz could possibly teach her, but she kept her opinion to herself.

"There are as many ways to successfully do missionary work as there are missionaries," he continued. "And I'm sure if you continue to be patient and exercise Christlike love, you will find that the spirit in your companionship will improve as will your success in finding those souls who are looking for the truth."

"I hope you're right," Amanda said without much conviction. The president meant well, she was sure, but evidently, he really didn't understand.

* * *

February 10, 2009

Dear Amanda,

Gosh, I can't believe it's been over a month since I last wrote you. I'm sorry you were worried, but there really isn't anything wrong. Just a lot of stuff going on right now. I'm taking a statistics class, and you wouldn't believe how time-consuming that can be. Plus, I'm thinking of switching my major. I was leaning toward law, but now I'm not so sure. It seems like there are all these options open to me, and I need to figure out what I really want to do with my life.

I'm sorry you're having so many struggles right now, but I'm sure if you just pray about it, everything will eventually work out. Oh, Happy Valentine's Day too!

Love,
Jake

Several weeks had passed since the zone conference, and as far as Amanda could tell, nothing had changed. They were making regular visits to some part-member families, but no one had been willing to take the lessons.

Her frustration with Sister Schultz was increasing daily, and she wasn't sure if she could endure the four more weeks until her companion went home.

One afternoon they were driving down Highway 880 when Amanda suggested tracting for the hundredth time but, as usual, her companion had other ideas.

"Let's go to the SCU campus. We're sure to have more luck there," Sister Schultz said as she turned into the parking lot.

"What would we do? Just wander around the campus looking for people to teach?"

"Something like that," Sister Schultz said. "You always get so antsy when you don't have everything under control, don't you? Just relax and watch."

They parked near the student center, and Amanda glared at her companion's back as she followed her in. Sister Schultz walked through the facility, passing the bookstore, food court, and copy center, never slowing her pace.

"We can't preach in here," Amanda said glancing around for anyone that looked like campus security. "This is a Catholic university. They'll kick us out in no time."

"We won't be preaching," her companion said over her shoulder. "Just finding. This will be great, and I know you're going to be amazed."

At last they reached their destination: SCU's student hangout, the Bronco. Though it was midafternoon, the gaming area had no windows and sat in semidarkness. Pool tables and other forms of mindless entertainment littered the place. Amanda looked around with an inward groan. These places always filled her with disgust. They were dirty and smelled like body odor and stale popcorn.

Sister Schultz walked through the room, heading for a huge table in the center. "This is it!" she announced.

"This is what?"

"This is an air-hockey table, and it's going to help us build our teaching pool."

Amanda stared at her companion in disbelief. "You're serious, aren't you? And just how is this game supposed to help us?"

"Come on, Sister Kelly. Use your imagination. It's simple really. A friend of mine who served in Chicago a few years back told me about it, and I've been wanting to try it."

Amanda felt an uncomfortable knot in the pit of her stomach, a sure sign that this was a bad idea.

"You and I play until someone stops to watch us. Then we say, 'Hey, how 'bout a game? To make it more interesting, let's make a little bet.' Then they say, 'Sure, what do you want to play for?' Then we say, 'We're missionaries from The Church of Jesus Christ, yada yada, and if we win, you let us share a short message about Jesus Christ with you. And if you win . . . then you don't have to listen to us.'"

"Are you nuts?" asked Amanda. "This is like gambling, and I'm sure there's got to be some mission rule against it."

"Gambling? Oh, come on. Be serious. Just relax for a minute and look outside the box. My friend said that they had a lot of success. Besides, what do we have to lose? At best, we find someone to teach, and at worst we get to play a little air hockey."

Amanda glanced around. Since school was in session, the center was mostly empty except for a few long-haired boys, one sporting a nose ring, who were taking turns at the Dance Dance Revolution, their bodies moving rhythmically as they tried to keep up with the arrows on the monitor and the screaming voices on the soundtrack. "And where are these prospective investigators supposed to come from?"

"Have a little faith."

Before Amanda could respond, Sister Schultz pulled a roll of quarters out of her purse and fed them into the machine, causing the air fan to hum loudly.

"Hey," Amanda said, "those are for laundry tomorrow."

"This will be a lot more fun than laundry. Trust me. Here's your pusher and there's our puck. Have you ever played air hockey?" she asked.

"Maybe once on an incredibly boring date," Amanda said, deflating more with each passing moment.

"Good! You take that end, and I'll take this one. Let's get started."

Amanda stood frozen, feeling trapped. She couldn't walk out and leave her companion alone, but at the same time an unmistakably bad feeling gnawed away at her.

"Come on," urged Sister Schultz, bouncing the thin plastic disk off the sides of the table. "I can't play alone."

With no other option, Amanda slowly took her place at the other end of the table and returned the puck halfheartedly.

They'd been playing for about fifteen minutes when a young man walked up and watched them. He wore a Bronco's T-shirt, and a leather money pouch hung from his waist, so Amanda assumed he worked there.

"I think you need to play someone at your own level," he remarked, looking sympathetically at Amanda. "It's supposed to be fun."

"So I hear," she said.

"Do you play?" Sister Schultz asked.

"Yeah, some. When it's quiet."

"Well, let me challenge you to a game."

"All right, but the game is on me," he said, reaching into his pouch and pulling out two tokens. The table began to vibrate again, and the first puck slipped onto the surface.

"Before we play, how about a little bet?"

"Sorry, I only play for fun," he said as he set the puck in motion.

They played two games in a row, but his eyes kept straying to where Amanda stood watching. There was something about the way he looked at her, eyes all slippery and smile all oily, that gave Amanda the creeps.

"Who are you ladies?" he asked. "The secret air-hockey police testing out the tables?" He looked closely at their name tags, trying to read them in the dim light. "Sister Kelly and Sister Schultz. Hey, you're not nuns, are you?" he asked, raising his eyebrows.

"No, no," Sister Schultz said. "We're missionaries from The Church of Jesus Christ of Latter-day Saints. Have you ever heard of us?"

A siren sounded from one of the games behind them, but he didn't take his eyes off the sisters. "No, I don't think so." He leaned back against the table. "That's a religion, right? Or is it a sect or a cult?"

"We're Christians," Amanda said stiffly.

"As missionaries, we are serving in the San Jose area for eighteen months, sharing a message about Jesus Christ," Sister Schultz said, her voice animated.

"I'm Eric." He let his eyes drift over Amanda's slim figure. "So, do you two have boyfriends?"

"We're missionaries," Sister Schultz said, smiling at him. "We can't date while we're on missions."

"Oh, come on, now," he said, moving closer to Amanda. "It's not like you're prisoners or anything, right?"

Amanda took a few steps backward. Didn't Sister Schultz get it? They needed to leave, and fast.

"You know there's a lot about the Church of Jesus Christ that you probably don't know." Sister Schultz pulled out her planner.

Eric's full attention was on Amanda. She backed into the wall, where he placed his arms on either side of her, trapping her with his body. His face was so close that Amanda could feel the moist air of his breath on her neck. She tried to slide out, but he lowered his arm to encircle her waist.

"Let me go!" she cried, twisting to get loose. He laughed and tightened his grip.

"Hey," Sister Schultz said. "You can't do that."

Eric looked over his shoulder. "You'll have to wait your turn. But don't worry. There's plenty of me to go around."

Amanda managed to free one arm and dig her nails into his chest, but Eric pushed in closer, wedging her hand firmly between their bodies.

She was beginning to panic as he brought his face closer to hers. "No!" she said, struggling to break free.

Suddenly, he yelped, swore, fell on the floor, curled up into a ball, and groaned. Amanda turned to Sister Schultz, who was bent over, trying to catch her breath.

"Four years of karate and two older brothers," Sister Schultz said. "One kick to the back of the kneecap and a follow-up side punch. Works every time." She stood up and looked toward the front door. "Come on, let's get out of here."

She got no argument from Amanda, who was ready to run back to the car.

It took every ounce of self-control Amanda had to keep her temper under control until they were out of the student center and in the car. She didn't know who she was angrier at, the hustler they'd left on the floor or her companion, who'd gotten her into this situation in the first place.

As soon as the car door shut, Amanda turned on the other girl with barely controlled rage. Her voice went deathly quiet. "I want you to listen to me. I've had it, and I don't care if you are senior companion. We're not going to work like this anymore. Do you hear me?"

Sister Schultz stared, her mouth hanging open.

"I'm not wasting another minute of my mission playing your stupid games, and I'm not buying another one of your stupid excuses. Either we do it right and start being real missionaries, or we go to the mission office right now and I tell President Edwards that I refuse to work with you."

"What are you talking about?" Sister Schultz asked.

Now it was Amanda's turn to stare in stunned amazement. "What am I talking about? We have no investigators. You won't tract. You talk to your mother for about two hours every week, and you get us into dangerous situations like with that guy just now and those construction workers the other day. I'm sick and tired of it!"

"You're blaming that scene in the Bronco on me?" Sister Schultz said, the bewilderment in her face turning to anger. "I'm the one that rescued you. It's not my fault you attract men like a cat in heat!"

Amanda's breath whooshed out of her. "What?"

Sister Schultz shrugged. "I'm sure you don't do your hair and your makeup so carefully each morning just to impress me. Don't you think I know what you're doing? You think you're better than me." Sister Schultz shook her head. "You never listen to what I say, and you assume you're always right. Well, you're no different than the rest of us—just an ordinary human. Shocking, isn't it?"

Amanda sat speechless. She'd been the victim of her companion's poor choices since they'd arrived in the area, but somehow the tables had turned, and she wasn't sure how. Sister Schultz made it sound like everything was Amanda's fault.

She had barely buckled her seat belt when her companion jammed the car into gear and sped out of the parking lot. Neither spoke on the drive home. As soon as they arrived at their apartment, Sister Schultz marched into the bedroom and slammed the door.

Amanda paced the living room. She'd told herself that she was justified in her appraisal of the situation. Sister Schultz was self-centered, disobedient, and an all-around bad missionary. The family Amanda was searching for was still out there somewhere, and she was stuck messing around with a trunky companion.

Sinking down into the couch, she considered her companion's accusations. *Is that how she sees me?*

The other girl's words hurt, and the idea that there might be another side to their problems, an angle she hadn't seen before, stabbed at Amanda's conscience. She'd never actually tried to understand her companion. She'd preached to her, judged her, and put up with her, but never once had Amanda tried to find out what made her companion tick.

She considered the rest of Sister Schultz's words. Amanda could admit that looking her best every day was important to her. It made her feel more prepared. And she had assumed that Schultz would understand that feeling, even if she didn't share it. But Amanda could see now how someone might interpret her actions as primping.

She and Sister Schultz needed to talk, of that Amanda was sure. She got up and headed toward the bedroom, determined to work things out.

Sister Schultz was sitting on the bed, her journal open in her lap. She didn't look up as Amanda came in and sat down. Neither one said a word for several minutes.

"I didn't know I was making your life so miserable," Sister Schultz finally said in a quiet voice.

Amanda was grateful for this olive branch. "Apparently I wasn't doing any better."

She struggled trying to think of something to say, something that would bridge all the anger and hurt between them. Finally she said, "I want to ask you a question, but I don't want you to think I'm nagging. I just want to understand, okay?"

"Okay," Sister Schultz said, her voice almost a whisper.

"Why won't you go tracting? I know you're not shy because you're always approaching strangers in other places and telling them about the gospel. I just don't get it."

Sister Schultz was silent, and Amanda was afraid that she wouldn't answer.

The silence continued for a good minute until finally Schultz spoke softly. "My third area was this part of San Jose that was really bad. I mean the spirit on the street was bad, and even the ward was weird. We had maybe one dinner appointment a month, and the members were actually rude to the few investigators we managed to get to church."

"How awful," Amanda said.

"Yeah. I mean our ward is a little stuck-up, but these guys would actually get up and move if an investigator smelled like cigarettes. I don't know what the problem was, but my companion and I had to tract for hours and hours and hours. There was nothing else for us to do. People threw stuff at us from passing cars, spit on us at doors. This one lady followed us down the street, swearing and warning everyone to stay away or they would all go to hell. By the end of the day, my feet would ache, my head would ache, and my soul would ache. But the next morning, we had to get up and do it all again."

Tears began to form in Sister Schultz's eyes, and Amanda moved to sit next to her.

"For weeks and weeks it went on like that. It was the lowest point of my mission—of my whole life. And for all that humiliation and pain and effort, we didn't see one single baptism or even a good investigator. Just the thought of knocking on a door now makes me physically ill. Maybe I'm a terrible missionary, but I thought . . . there has got to be a better way to share the gospel than that."

It had never occurred to Amanda that her companion was afraid to tract, and from what she'd just said, Sister Schultz certainly had reason. "It must have been horrible," Amanda said as a flash of comprehension suddenly filled her mind. "I'm sorry."

"You're sorry? For what?" Sister Schultz asked in surprise.

"I'm sorry that I misjudged you and waited so long to really talk to you."

"I think we've both misjudged each other," said Sister Schultz, wiping a tear from her eye. "You know, I go home in less than a month and, to be honest, I feel like most of my mission has been kind of a waste of time—like I haven't made a difference in anyone's life."

Amanda pondered her own experiences. "I know that feeling; it's scary, isn't it?"

"I just don't want to leave and feel like it was all for nothing."

Amanda sighed. "I don't know if my mission's made much of a difference to anyone else, but I do know that it's made a difference in me."

It was true. Amanda was a better person now than she'd been only a few short months ago.

Sister Schultz looked up. "Do you think that's enough?" she asked.

"It's a start. But you know, it isn't too late. You can go home on a high note if you want. If we both worked really hard . . ." She let the words trail off as a look of discouragement passed across her companion's face.

"I'm not sure if I can. I mean, I'm still me."

"And I'm still me," Amanda said, laughing a little. "But if we work together, I bet we could do it."

The sudden sound of the phone ringing startled Amanda. She jumped up and hurried in to get it.

When she came back, Sister Schultz was pacing the floor. "Is everything okay?" she asked.

"I think I owe you another apology," Amanda said.

"For what?"

"For doubting your finding methods. That was Elder Criddle on the phone. It seems that one of the men from the construction site the other day actually called in on the pass-along card. He wants us to come talk to him and his family next week."

"I can't believe it," said Sister Schultz.

"Well, believe it. We now have our first investigator."

* * *

It was early morning, and Amanda was drying her hair at the mirror. "I'll tell you what," Sister Schultz called from the bedroom. "If you go without makeup today, I agree to do two hours of tracting."

"No way," Amanda responded. "You have no idea how awful I look without makeup."

"Hello . . . I live with you."

Amanda laughed. "Okay, I have to do mascara, but I'll skip the eyeliner and shadow in return for one hour of tracting and one hour of handing out pass-along cards in the park. Deal?"

"Deal."

It had taken a bit of time, but Amanda and Sister Schultz had begun to feel the Spirit increase in their companionship. Schultz agreed to do companion study as long as Amanda gave her extra time for personal study. And Amanda learned to appreciate her companion's sense of humor and creative contacting ideas.

"But before we go out, we need to stop by Sister Taylor's apartment," Sister Schultz said. "She left a message on the answering machine asking us to come over."

Brenda Taylor answered the door after their first knock. "Sisters, come in. I'm so excited I can hardly stand it."

"What is it?" Amanda asked.

Sister Taylor took a deep breath. "So, after that Relief Society lesson you guys gave on finding people who were ready to receive the gospel, I came home and I just felt like I wanted to do something. So I prayed and fasted for an opportunity."

"Good for you," Sister Schultz said. "I wasn't sure anyone was listening."

It was still difficult for the sisters to get cooperation from the ward in finding referrals. But they were getting more dinner invitations, and Amanda was hopeful that eventually the members would catch the missionary spirit.

"I was over at the school helping out in my daughter's fifth-grade class last week, and the teacher was talking about pioneers. She taught that Brigham Young had led the Mormons to Utah. So I told her that my great-great-great grandmother had traveled across the plains to Utah and that I had a copy of a journal her mother wrote during the trip."

Amanda could feel the Spirit spreading through the room, and Sister Taylor's face was beaming. "So then what happened?"

"Well, one thing led to another, and I told her about the Book of Mormon, and she said she wanted to read it. Yesterday I brought a copy to school with my testimony written in the front cover."

Brenda wiped a tear from her eye. "I don't know if anything will happen, but it felt so good and I couldn't wait to tell you guys."

Amanda reached out and hugged their neighbor. Maybe she and Sister Schultz were finally getting their member missionary message out.

* * *

March 4, 2009

Dear Jake,

I think winter is officially over and spring has come. The hills are covered in green grass and bright yellow flowers. Even the highways are lined with wildflowers. There are these gorgeous orange poppies that grow everywhere, but they are the state flower, so you can't pick them. It's hard to believe that Provo is still buried under a foot and a half of snow.

My companion goes home next week, and I'm really going to miss her. We actually have three investigators as well. Finally!

Jake, I need to ask you something. We are still okay, aren't we? I didn't write something that hurt your feelings, did I? It's just that you haven't written in a long time. I love you so much, and I miss hearing from you. Your support means everything to me.

Love forever,
Amanda

Amanda had her planner spread out on the table, and Sister Schultz sat next to her.

"I wish that Max and his wife would commit to be baptized before I leave," Schultz said. "It would make such a cool homecoming talk—you know, finding him at that construction site and then having him call for the lessons. If I could say he agreed to be baptized, that would be so awesome."

Amanda pushed her hair behind her ears. "I know. I wish he would too, but it's tough giving up the cigarettes."

"Let's at least try to get one more lesson in before I leave on Wednesday."

Amanda slid her finger across the page. "We could go by their house on Tuesday night after our dinner with the Sanchez family."

The last month had been a bittersweet experience for Amanda. On the one hand, she and Sister Schultz had worked harder than ever trying to make up for all the time they'd lost at the beginning. On the other hand, both sisters had developed a close bond that Amanda would never have imagined possible.

Amanda wondered why it had taken her so long to appreciate this young woman. *If I hadn't been so busy feeling self-righteous for all those weeks and misjudging her motives, we could have worked things out months ago.*

"Do you have all your stuff packed?" she asked.

Sister Schultz's parents were driving down to pick up their daughter and take her back to Montana. It was a good thing, too, because during the course of her eighteen months, Sister Schultz had accumulated more stuff than any airline would willingly ship. Amanda wondered if they'd have to rent a U-Haul.

"Pretty much," Sister Schultz said. "I wish I could stay longer. I begged and pleaded with the president to extend me a month, but he said it was time for me to leave. What am I going to do at home?"

Amanda laughed. "Whip those brothers of yours into shape."

"Yeah, someone has got to do it. Who did you say is coming out to take my place?"

"Sister Carlson," Amanda said. "She's been out about a month longer than me."

"Hopefully that means she won't be trunky," Sister Schultz said.

"Hopefully." Amanda smiled. "You don't suppose she knows karate, do you?"

"Sister Kelly, you and I both know there isn't another sister in the mission like me. You've had the best, so you'll have to put up with the rest."

Amanda smiled as she got up to get a glass of water. When she returned she found her companion lost in thought.

"Did you know I never had a baptism? Not even one during my whole mission."

Amanda shook her head. "I didn't know that."

"Yeah. Do you think it was still worth it? My coming out I mean?"

"A wise sister missionary once told me that some missionaries plant the seeds, some water and nurture them, and some pick the harvest, and it doesn't matter who does what, as long as it gets done. So, yeah, I think it was worth it."

Sister Schultz nodded her head. "Yeah, I think it was too."

Chapter Nine

March 11, 2009

Dear Amanda,

Everything is fine. You worry too much. I'm just way busy, that's all. School is crazy and some days I hardly have time to even check my e-mails. Plus, I've been out of stamps and haven't had time to get to the post office. Hope all is well with you.

Love,
Jake

SISTER LAUREN CARLSON WAS LOOKING forward to her next assignment. She'd always enjoyed going to new places and meeting new people. Sometimes her transfers went smoothly. Sometimes they didn't, like the time the office messed up and assigned her as junior companion to a sister who only spoke Korean. Either way, Lauren always found that transfers were an adventure.

"So, Elder Brunk," she said to the AP driving the minivan. "Now that you're an assistant to the president, does that mean I have to call you *sir*?"

"How about Elder Brunk, the High and Mighty?" suggested Elder Van, the senior AP.

Elder Brunk was one of the first missionaries Lauren had met when she first arrived in the mission, and she'd always enjoyed his quick wit and his dedication to the gospel. She wasn't the least bit surprised when he was called to take Elder Criddle's place as AP after Criddle went home. Still, she couldn't resist the opportunity to rub it in a little.

"Or maybe His Worthiness, Elder B?" She laughed as they pulled up to the apartment complex.

"Let's just stick with He Who Knows Everything." Elder Brunk shifted the vehicle into park. "That should about cover it, don't you think?'

They gathered her luggage from the back of the van and carried it up the stairs.

"What have you got in here?" Brunk asked. "The original gold plates?"

"That and the sword of Laban," Lauren responded. "Come on, they aren't that heavy. Put your back into it."

"This is it." Elder Van pointed toward an apartment on the second floor.

By the time they reached the door, it was already open and Sister Kelly was waiting outside. Lauren studied the sister with interest. She'd been told that her new companion was pretty, and she'd imagined a fluffy blond with big blue eyes all dressed in pink. Nothing could have been further from the truth. The sister at the door was attractive in an elegant and sophisticated sort of way.

Elder Brunk groaned as he climbed the last stair. "And the door is open and waiting," he said, dropping the suitcases with a loud thump. "Now that's what I call service."

Lauren beamed. "We're missionaries, and that means we have inspiration in everything. Didn't you know that?"

"Oh, is that how it works?" asked Elder Van. "I thought it was 'perspiration' in everything."

"Maybe for you," Elder Brunk shot back.

Sister Kelly smiled a little at the banter, but Lauren noticed that the pleasure didn't reach her eyes. *Is something wrong?* she wondered.

In the past, Lauren had always gotten along well with her companions right from the start, even the Korean sister. *It may take a little more effort to get to know this one,* Lauren decided.

"Hey, thanks for the ride. Try not to screw up any transfers, okay?" she said as the elders turned to leave.

"Yeah, well, with this guy," Elder Van said, elbowing his new companion, "I can't make any promises."

Lauren moved the last of her bags into the living room just as a woman came out of the bathroom.

"Sister Carlson, this is Brenda Taylor, our neighbor. She's been staying here with me since Sister Schultz left with her parents."

"Nice to meet you," Lauren said, reaching out to shake Brenda's hand. "Are you in our ward?"

"That I am." The other woman laughed. "Well, I'd better get back to my place."

"Thank you so much," Sister Kelly said.

Once Brenda left, Lauren shut the door and turned to her new companion. "I've been really looking forward to meeting you. Why don't you show me where the bedroom is, and we can visit while I unpack. I have all kinds of questions."

Sister Kelly led the way without speaking as Lauren followed.

Tossing her suitcase onto the top of the bare twin mattress, Lauren snapped open the locks and began moving clothes from the suitcase to the dresser drawer. "I understand that you've been out about five months. Is that right?" she asked.

"Six months," Sister Kelly said, then took a deep breath. "I need to say something and I'm not sure how to put it, so I'm going to jump right in and say it."

Lauren stopped unpacking and turned, giving Sister Kelly her full attention.

"Santa Clara has proven to be a challenging area to work in. We've had very few investigators, and the only way we've found those is by working hard. We've had to tract twelve hours a day because we can't get the members to help us out. And we've had to follow every single mission rule to the letter so that we are worthy of the Lord's blessings. This isn't a fun area, but I think it can be successful. My question is, are you willing to work hard with me? Because I refuse to waste any more of the Lord's time."

So that's what's eating her, thought Lauren. *She's worried that I'm not going to work hard enough.* She began to chuckle. *Evidently my reputation didn't precede me.*

Sister Kelly's face turned red. "I don't know what you think is so funny."

"I'm sorry," Lauren said. "I'm not laughing at you, really. Actually, I think it's great that you want to start our companionship right off with an open communication policy. I agree with you one-hundred percent. I'm here to work and serve the Lord, and I'm delighted that you are, too. In fact, this unpacking can wait. Let's find some missionary work to do this afternoon. What do you suggest?"

For a minute, Sister Kelly seemed at a loss for words, and then she gave a self-conscious little smile. "How do you feel about tracting?"

"You've never tracted until you've tracted with me," Lauren quipped.

* * *

As they drove out to the street that Amanda had chosen to tract, her thoughts wandered. She hadn't meant to come down so hard on her new companion, but when she'd stood at the door watching Sister Carlson get out of the minivan, laughing and joking with the elders, she'd panicked. She could feel her cheeks warming. Sister Schultz had only been gone a few hours, and already Amanda was misjudging her new companion. Evidently she still needed to work on that. And what about the family she was looking for? Were they still out there waiting?

Sister Carlson flipped through the area book, trying to familiarize herself with the ward. She was almost the same height as Amanda and had long auburn hair—not as dark as Jake's but with the same strong red highlights. It bounced at her shoulders as she walked. The freckles that covered her nose and cheeks wrinkled whenever she laughed, which was often. Amanda couldn't help but be infected by her comp's sense of joy.

Amanda parked the car and the sisters got out. The area she'd chosen to tract out was in a less affluent part of town with small, run-down homes and huge old gnarled trees that had been growing there for years.

"Sister Kelly, how many different door approaches do you know?"

Amanda shrugged her shoulders. "Maybe three or four. Why?"

"I'll bet that I can come up with a door approach using any word you give me."

"What do you mean?"

"It's a game," Sister Carlson explained. "Here, I'll show you. Say a word. Any word at all."

"Okay, *Jesus*."

"No, no. That's too easy. Give me a different word. An unusual one."

They stopped and knocked on a door, but after a few moments when no one answered, they moved on.

"Fine. My word is *prototype*," Amanda said.

"Good choice. Okay, let me see. 'Hello. Did you know that this earth life is a prototype of how we are meant to live with our Father in Heaven? We'd like to come in and share a short message with you.' Get the idea? Now you try."

"Me?" Amanda laughed. "This is your game."

"Oh, come on. Just try it. Your word is *two*—I like the number two."

Amanda concentrated, barely noticing the sweet fragrance of orange blossoms coming from a nearby yard.

"All right. Okay. 'Did you know that God the Father and Jesus Christ are two separate individuals?' How's that?"

"Not bad," Sister Carlson pronounced solemnly. "For a beginner." She laughed, breaking her somber expression.

An elderly man answered the next door and summarily dismissed them when he learned they were missionaries. They passed several homes with tiny but well-cared-for front yards followed by an empty lot that had been allowed to overgrow into a jungle of weeds.

"Now it's your turn to pick a word," Sister Carlson said.

"How about *tree house*?" Amanda asked, feeling mischievous.

"Oh, now that's a good one. Let's see . . . How's this? 'Did you know that after we die, there are three heavens or degrees of glory that we can inherit? One is the glory of a tree house, one the glory of a mobile home, and one the glory of a mansion.'"

Amanda groaned, trying hard not to laugh. "Isn't that stretching it just a bit?"

"That's the object of the game. The scriptures teach that everything testifies of Christ and helps us to appreciate and remember Him. We just make a game of looking for that connection."

They knocked on five more doors without success before reaching the end of the block. It was Sister Carlson's turn to take the next one as they rounded the corner.

"I bet this will be the home of a young woman," Sister Carlson said as they walked up the path. "She'll have blond curly hair and a gray tabby cat rubbing up against her leg."

"Excuse me?"

"Haven't you ever tried to guess who lives in a house before they open door?"

"No," admitted Amanda.

"Well, maybe you haven't done enough tracting," she said, arching her eyebrows dramatically.

Not the way you do it, Amanda thought, smiling.

A faint rustling from within the house followed their knock, and the door seemed to open by itself. It took Amanda a moment to make out the small, dark-skinned child, half hidden in the shadowy interior.

Squatting down until she was at eye level with the child, Amanda said, "Is your mommy home?"

He nodded his head and promptly stuck his thumb into his mouth. He couldn't have been more than three.

"Can you get her?"

He nodded again and then turned and ran back into the house.

Amanda and Sister Carlson waited for several minutes at the open front door, but neither the child nor an adult returned.

Sister Carlson took a step into the doorway and looked around. "Do you think he's okay? There's got to be an adult here somewhere, right?"

"I'm sure there must be. Maybe we should ring the bell again."

"We'd just get the kid." Sister Carlson took another step into the room. "Hello?" she called out. "Is anyone home?"

Amanda followed her into the cool interior. The house was small, and most of the blinds were still closed over the windows blocking the glare of the early afternoon sun.

The entry led to a short hallway. To the left was a kitchen. A glass-topped table and two chairs were visible through the open doorway. To the right was a small living room with just enough space for a chair and small couch. Several prints of elongated African women in native dress hung on the walls.

Now that they were inside, faint sounds could be heard emanating from behind a closed door in the hall. The rhythm and tone of the voice suggested a female talking on the phone. A few yards away from the sisters, sitting lotus-style on the rug was the little boy. He held a truck in one hand and a toy screwdriver in the other.

"Hey," Amanda called out and he looked up at the sisters. "We need to talk to your mommy. Could you get her?"

He smiled, his cheeks still chubby with baby fat, and gathered the toys in one hand using the other to push himself to a standing position. Once he'd gotten his balance, he leaned against the door to his right. It opened under the weight of his shoulder, and he disappeared inside.

The woman's words were audible now. "Can I call you back, Pat? I have a little guy who needs me. Okay, bye then." Her voice became softer. "Josh, baby, you about ready for a snack?"

The child murmured in response.

A moment later, the little boy came out the door, his hand firmly pulling on the woman's blouse. "Okay, baby, I'm coming."

At first she didn't seem to notice the two sister missionaries who stood in the entryway, but when she did the woman stopped in her tracks, pulling Josh more closely to her side. "Now what the heck are two white girls doing standing in my house?"

Amanda pointed to the little boy. "I'm sorry, but he opened the door, and we didn't want to leave until we let someone know."

"Oh, really?" The woman raised one eyebrow, a look of disbelief on her face. "He's never unlocked the dead bolt before."

"I'm sorry we scared you," Sister Carlson said.

It took several minutes for the sisters to explain themselves, but by the time they had finished, the frown lines had left and the woman looked amused. "We're missionaries from The Church of Jesus Christ of Latter-day

Saints, and we are out today sharing a short message about Jesus Christ. Do you have a few minutes?"

"Well, since you're already in here, I guess it wouldn't hurt. I'm Kitiara, and you've already met my son, Joshua."

Kitiara was a few years older than Amanda. Her shiny black hair hung straight down to her jawbone where it curled slightly in toward her face. She had large full lips and deep brown eyes surrounded by thick lashes. Her jeans and oversized, untucked men's dress shirt gave her full figure an air of casual comfort.

Joshua, who now sat on his mother's lap, stared intently at Amanda. Kitiara glanced down at him. "I think you have an admirer," she said.

"He's a darling. Is Josh your only child?"

Kitiara hugged her son a little tighter, a sad look coming into her eyes. "We lost his father two years ago in Iraq. He was in the army."

"I'm so sorry," Sister Carlson said.

"We're managing, aren't we?" She kissed the top of the child's head. "Josh was only fourteen months old when it happened. I'm just glad David got to spend a little time with his son before . . ."

For a moment the woman didn't speak, and Amanda sensed that she was struggling to gather her emotions—something she'd probably had to do a lot over the past couple of years.

"So," she continued after a moment, "you said you wanted to tell me something about Jesus?"

"We do," Sister Carlson said and then began by recounting Christ's teachings in the Old and New Worlds. When she mentioned the Book of Mormon, a look of understanding came over Kitiara's face.

"You're Mormons, then?" she said. "I know a Mormon family. Maybe you do too. Randy and Samantha Thompson? They live in Cupertino."

Both sisters shook their heads.

"That's too bad. Randy and his family are really amazing people."

Kitiara had met Randy through work. "I'm a video graphic designer," she explained. "It lets me work at home and stay with my son."

She shifted the child on her lap.

"Randy's a composer and does music and vocal background for some of the demos I create. We've worked together for years. In fact, we were in the middle of a project when I lost David." Her voice cracked as she said her husband's name. "They have a bunch of children. Family is important to them, and he understood how hard it was for us."

"I can imagine," Amanda said in agreement.

"Then, about four months ago, Randy and his wife lost their youngest baby. It was tragic. She hadn't been sick or anything, but one night they put her to bed and the next morning she was gone."

"Sudden infant death syndrome?" Sister Carlson asked.

"That's what they said. She was so little. Only six months old. It was terrible."

Joshua climbed off of his mother's lap and wandered into the kitchen.

"He and his family had been so good to us. I sent flowers and attended the funeral. It was very sad, of course, but I was amazed at how peaceful the family appeared. A few weeks later I asked Randy how he was holding up. He said that some days were harder than others but that he took comfort in his church's teaching that his family would be together forever. He said he knew that they would see their little girl again and would be able to have her for always."

A tear formed at the corner of Kitiara's eye, and she brushed it away quickly.

"I've thought a lot about what he said. I believe David still exists some-where." She waved her hand in the air. "And I admit it would be wonderful to think that someday we could see him again and be with him. But if it's not true, what would be the point of deluding myself? How can a person ever know for sure?"

Joshua returned from the kitchen with a graham cracker and climbed back up on his mother's lap to eat it.

Amanda could hardly wait to bear her testimony, and as soon as Kitiara had finished talking, she leaned in and met her gaze. "Your husband still lives and loves you. I know that you and your son can be reunited with him again. If you'll let us, we can teach you how to find this out for yourself."

Kitiara looked at the photo of her husband on the wall for a few min-utes. Finally she answered, "I'd like that."

* * *

Kitiara had agreed to meet with them later that week, and the sisters left her home intoxicated with the joy of the Spirit.

"Was that golden or what?" Sister Carlson asked.

"Definitely," Amanda said. "It's like the Lord directed us to her at exact-ly the right time."

"She's sharp." Sister Carlson jotted the woman's name and contact information on their list of investigators. "And that little boy is the cutest thing I've ever seen."

"Do you think it was a coincidence that today was the day Josh learned how to unlock the front door?"

"Do you even have to ask?"

Amanda sent up a silent prayer of thanks. "No."

* * *

When they got back to the apartment, there was a message on the answering machine from the elders inviting them to a district activity at the church.

"We're going to play basketball and have lunch. If we all pitched in some money, could you bring the food? Anything will be fine. Chocolate chip cookies, even, if it's not too much trouble."

Amanda groaned as she deleted the message. "That always bugs me."

"What?"

"At almost every district activity I've attended, the elders seem to think that because we're female we should be responsible for all the cooking. Just once it would be nice to go to a district activity and not have to bring the food."

"Trust me, I've eaten food the elders cooked." Her companion made a sour face. "It's a lot better if we do it. I remember one activity where the elders made sandwiches with peanut butter, chocolate chips, bananas, and tiny marshmallows on raisin bread. I spent the whole night running in and out of the bathroom."

"You have a point."

Sister Carlson kicked off her shoes and sat down on the couch. "The elders are young and sometimes a little immature, but all in all they're pretty good guys."

"True." Amanda sat down next to her companion.

"And we're kind of lucky to work with them," Sister Carlson continued.

"How do you mean?"

"Think about it. For two years, each of these guys is living as close to Christ as he probably ever has. They're at the top of their game spiritually, so to speak, and we get to see it. Not even their own parents get to know them like this. It's kind of an honor."

It was refreshing to hear a sister missionary with such a positive outlook on the elders, and it made Amanda respect her new companion even more.

"So when is this activity?" Sister Carlson asked.

"A week from Monday on our preparation day. Why?"

"Just wondered. Is Hoff still the district leader here?"

Amanda shook her head. "He got transferred out about a month ago. Our new DL is Elder Castro. Have you ever met him?"

"Castro? Yeah, I know him. He came out the same time I did. We teased him because he is so hairy. Have you seen his arms and legs? He even has hair on his knuckles."

Amanda laughed. "Yes, that's him. He's a good leader though."

"That for sure. Even in the MTC you could tell he was going to make a great missionary."

Sister Carlson dropped down onto the couch. "Not a bad day," she said. "I get transferred into a new area, teach my junior companion the finer aspects of tracting, and find a golden family in the process." She grabbed a throw pillow and tossed it at Amanda. "Now, the big question is, what's for dinner? Mac and cheese or Chinese noodles?"

Amanda caught the pillow but didn't answer. She was thinking of their new investigator and her dark-eyed little boy. And she wondered if his face seemed somehow familiar.

Chapter Ten

March 23, 2008

Dear Jake,

Can you believe it's been eight months already? Next month I'll celebrate my hump day. The sisters don't cut a tie in half like the elders, but Sister Carlson and I are going out for Chinese food to celebrate. In some ways it seems like the time has flown by amazingly fast. I wonder if the second half will go by as quickly.

We are finally getting some investigators. Yay! And we met a woman and her child the other day that I think are really golden. My companion and I are becoming great friends. She's from Kaysville, so hopefully we can continue our friendship even after our missions.

I think about you all the time, and you have no idea how much I miss you. I know that we are meant to be together, and I know that you feel the same way. I love you.

Love always,
Amanda

ON P-DAY, THE EARLY MORNING sun streamed through the kitchen window and across the table where Amanda sat flipping through a pile of mail. "Hey, Sister, guess what? We got a media referral."

The bathroom door opened, and her companion stuck out her head. "What did you say?" she asked, a toothbrush hanging from the corner of her mouth.

"A media referral," Amanda repeated, waving the card in the air next to her. "The office sent it with some other memos and stuff. It must have come in yesterday's mail. This is only the third one I've ever received."

Sister Carlson pulled the toothbrush out of her mouth. "Is it really? I've had dozens and dozens. Maybe the office has been saving them up till I got here. What did they request?"

Amanda turned the card over and looked closely. "The King James Bible for an Erica Smith," she read out loud. "I've never had a Bible request."

"That usually means someone who's interested in religion in general rather than the Church specifically." Sister Carlson pulled a curler out of her hair before heading back into the bathroom. "But let's not count her out yet. What does our schedule look like?"

Amanda picked up her planner. "We're pretty booked today with the district activity in the morning and correlation this afternoon. Maybe tomorrow. And speaking of the district, when Elder Castro called last night he said he got a new companion. A greenie who's been training down in Hollister for the past two months."

Sister Carlson came back out, combing the soft red waves of her hair.

"Constant change—that's my definition of mission life. Oh, and I finished the baking during personal study time this morning. It would be a tragedy if we didn't have enough homemade chocolate chip cookies."

"That's for sure." Amanda laughed.

* * *

The sisters pulled into the church parking lot at exactly eleven-thirty. As she turned off the engine, Amanda could see Elder Castro and his companion coming through the glass doors and heading toward them.

Elder Castro was golden skinned, with short, thick black hair and bushy eyebrows. He made a big show of looking at his watch. "So you made it."

"Of course we did," Amanda said, glancing down at her own watch. "Right on time too."

"And the chocolate chip cookies?" he asked, grabbing a grocery bag full of sodas from the trunk.

"Four dozen," Sister Carlson said. "All homemade."

"Here." Elder Castro shoved the sodas into the other missionary's arms. "This is Elder Hoyle. Elder, meet the sisters."

Amanda stepped up to greet him. Elder Hoyle was tall—she had to tip her head up to see him. "I'm Sister Kelly," she said, extending her hand. "Welcome to the district."

The young man smiled and tried shifting the bag of sodas around to free up his right hand, but as he did so, the bottom of the plastic bag ripped and the bottles slid through the hole. He managed to catch two, but a third hit the ground and rolled into the grass.

"Sorry," he said as an odd shade of orange-red slowly crept up his face.

"It's okay." Amanda laughed as she retrieved the soda from the lawn. "Let's just make sure we open this one last so I don't get a shower."

Sister Carlson handed two foil-covered pans to Elder Castro, who sniffed at them appreciatively. "Smells delicious. Enchiladas?"

"It's lasagna," Sister Carlson said, adding two brown paper–wrapped loaves of French bread to the load.

"Well, I knew it was something foreign."

Amanda held the church door as the two elders carried the food inside then returned to the car.

"Wow," Sister Carlson said.

"Wow, what?"

"Elder Hoyle. Don't tell me you didn't notice. He's got to be one of the best looking elders in the whole mission."

Amanda looked back at the spot where the young man had been standing moments before with his face bright red, holding two bottles of soda to his chest as if his life depended on it. "I hadn't noticed."

Sister Carlson rolled her eyes. "We may be missionaries, but that doesn't make us blind. What do you know about him?"

"Exactly as much as you do, which isn't a lot. Why?"

"Just wondering. I guess it's up to me to get the lowdown."

Amanda stopped in front of the church doors and turned to her companion. "Sister Carlson, do I need to worry about this?"

A light blush covered Sister Carlson's freckled cheeks, but her eyes shone. "Of course not. My heart is locked." She mimicked locking a key over her heart then pushed open the door and called over her shoulder. "But that doesn't mean I can't be curious about a person."

The lasagna went over well with all six of the elders in the district, and there was enough French bread and cookies to ensure that everyone had their fill. Someone brought a basketball, and as soon as the food was gone, the elders headed out on the gym floor.

Amanda sat on the stage with her legs dangling over the edge, watching the missionaries play and thinking about Jake. He always enjoyed a game of basketball. He wasn't really good, but his enthusiasm was contagious, and he was always welcome in a game.

Sister Carlson had gone out on the court with the elders. She'd never struck Amanda as the athletic type, and after watching her play, Amanda knew that her first impression was correct. The girl tried hard, but she couldn't really handle the ball. The elders didn't seem to mind though, and she was having a lot of fun.

Elder Hoyle moved about the court, waiting for his opportunity to shoot, and Amanda noticed that Sister Carlson had managed to spend quite a bit of time near him, her face animated and her mouth moving constantly. No doubt she was squeezing as much personal information from him between plays as she could.

Amanda took a moment to study the young missionary as he caught a pass and neatly sank a basket. He had a clean-cut, boy-next-door kind of look with dark wavy hair and the easy grace of an experienced athlete. *Probably played in high school,* she thought as he moved the ball skillfully across the court before passing it to one of the other elders. There was a certain charm in his features, Amanda admitted. Of course, he was probably annoyingly aware of it. Most good-looking guys were.

They'd been playing for over half an hour when Elder Castro took a break and made his way to where Amanda sat. He pulled himself up on the stage beside her, large damp stains already making their way down the neck and under the sleeves of his blue Nike shirt.

I'll bet he's roasting with all that hair, she thought, watching the elder mop his damp face with the end of his T-shirt.

He smiled at her and they both watched the game for a while. The ball went long, and one of the elders made a dive to try and catch it, but instead he got tangled up in his companion's legs and they both tumbled down in a heap.

After a few minutes Castro turned toward her. "Sister Kelly, the food was great. Thank you so much for bringing it."

"You're welcome." This was probably the third or fourth time Amanda had helped make lunch for a district activity, but never before had one of the elders ever thanked her for cooking. She was impressed. "Are you still on schedule to baptize that teenager you're teaching?"

He grimaced. "No. Brad is having some second thoughts. I don't think his parents approve, and they are giving him a hard time."

"I'm sorry," Amanda said. "I know how disappointing that can be."

He rubbed the palms of his hands on the knees of his pants. "Lately, it seems like we get so close with our investigators and then suddenly they back out."

They watched for a few more minutes in silence before he spoke again. "Do you ever wonder why it is that so many people have such a hard time recognizing the truth while others find their faith as natural as breathing?"

Amanda turned to him with interest. "I don't know. Maybe differences in personalities?"

Elder Castro shrugged his shoulders. "Maybe. Before my mission I took a psych class. They say that who we are is based on a mixture of the way we grew up and our genes. I'm sure that's true, but there's got to be more to it, like the spirit we come down with."

"Nature versus nurture," said Amanda, thinking of the children she'd seen walking around barefoot and dirty in some of the government-funded apartment buildings in the poorer areas of the mission. Some of them had parents who worked long hours to put food on the table, while others were the offspring of alcoholic or drug-addicted parents. What happened to a valiant spirit who was forced to live in that kind of environment?

He sighed. "I think, though, that in the end, it comes down to whether a person is willing to let the Savior come into their lives. If they open up and trust Him, then He will change both their hearts and their lives. And if they can't, then . . ."

Amanda lifted her eyebrows.

"Well, that's why I keep reminding myself," Castro continued, "that I can never judge who will and won't accept the gospel. I have to keep offering it to everyone."

Before she could pursue the subject further, Sister Carlson came up to join them. Her face was a little flushed, but she still smiled brightly.

"What are you two talking about so seriously?" She held her hair up off her neck with one hand, breathing heavily.

"Nothing much," Castro said as he jumped down from the stage. "Looks like I'd better get back to the game."

Amanda watched him jog onto the court and then turned to her companion. "Okay, so how did you make out?"

She leaned back against the stage. "With what?" Sister Carlson's eyes opened wide with such an innocent look that Amanda snorted.

"With what?" Amanda taunted. "With your investigation. Did you get any new information on Elder Hoyle?"

"I thought you weren't interested."

Amanda shook her head. "You're the one who said curiosity was a good thing."

"Yes, I did."

"Well?"

"All right, all right." Sister Carlson pushed herself up on the stage. "He converted to the Church a little over three years ago, and his family lives in Chicago. I don't think there's a girl back home—at least he wouldn't admit to one—and after his mission he's planning on attending BYU."

Amanda was impressed. "You got all that out on the court?"

"I know. It's a natural talent."

Just then, a wild throw caused the basketball to come flying their way, and Sister Carlson managed to catch it. "Careful, you guys!" she said, then, turning to her companion, she winked. "Looks like they need me back in the game."

* * *

Amanda consulted the map in her hand and compared it to the card in her lap as she and her companion drove down the street. They were in a part of town that they usually avoided. Several hole-in-the-wall bars separated by run-down apartment buildings and small mom-and-pop shops lined the street. "It should be somewhere on the next block."

She squinted her eyes against the sun and tried to read the numbers on the buildings as they passed. A homeless woman pushed her shopping cart overflowing with soda cans and other odds and ends along the street while a group of teenage boys hung out on a corner sharing their smokes.

"What's her name again?" asked Sister Carlson.

Amanda picked up the referral and read, "Erica Smith, and it says she works nights, so it's best to catch her during the day."

They'd tried to make an appointment by calling the number listed on the request form, but the phone line had been disconnected.

"I don't feel very safe here," Sister Carlson said, checking to make sure her door was locked.

"I know," Amanda agreed.

"There it is, on the right. And a free parking spot in front. Talk about luck."

Sister Carlson slid the car up to the curb, and they both got out.

Amanda glanced around nervously. This was the kind of neighborhood where you needed to keep your eyes open.

Eventually they found themselves standing in front of the battered second-floor apartment door. Sister Carlson winked at Amanda. "Your turn for the door approach," she said, stepping back a pace.

Amanda swallowed and then gave the door a tentative knock.

It took a few minutes before anyone responded, but at last the door was opened by a young woman in a green-and-blue checked robe who stared at the sisters with a look of confusion on her face. It was evident that she'd been sleeping; her long dark curly hair hung in a frizzed mass about her head, and the remains of what looked like heavy dark makeup were smeared around her hazel eyes.

Amanda guessed her age to be somewhere around twenty-four or twenty-five but with a hardness about her features that contradicted her youth. For a few moments no one said a word. At last Sister Carlson stepped forward.

"We're sister missionaries from The Church of Jesus Christ of Latter-day Saints, and we're delivering the King James Bible you requested. You're Erica Smith, right?"

The woman rubbed her eyes with her hand. "I . . . uh . . ."

"May we come in?" Sister Carlson continued, stepping forward.

The woman stepped back from the doorway automatically as Sister Carlson walked into the apartment. Amanda followed.

Erica's senses seemed to have suddenly cleared. She appeared to be having second thoughts about allowing the two missionaries into her home. "I'm busy now, so just give me the book, then you can . . ."

"We'll stay a minute," interrupted Sister Carlson. "Why don't you go get dressed? We can wait."

Amanda stared at her companion in surprise. She'd never seen Sister Carlson be so pushy.

Erica hesitated, considering the offer. "I guess that will be all right. I'll be back."

As the bedroom door closed behind the young woman, Amanda turned to her companion. "What are you doing?" she whispered.

Sister Carlson shrugged her shoulders. "We're supposed to be here. I can feel it. Can't you?"

Amanda's eyes moved from a pile of laundry sitting in the corner that consisted of thong panties and black lacy bras to a pair of handcuffs on the table next to a half-full bottle of amber liquid with a Johnny Walker Scotch label on the front. The room smelled of stale cigarette smoke and sour food. "No, I don't think I can."

"Not over there." Sister Carlson got up and walked toward the front door. "Look over here."

Amanda followed her companion to a small end table sitting in the shadows. All she saw was a dusty paperback novel resting on the table's edge, but upon closer examination, her eyes widened in surprise. "Is that what I think it is?"

Sister Carlson nodded. "A Book of Mormon. I saw it when she first opened the door. Now do you understand?"

"What are you two doing?"

Amanda turned around with a guilty start.

Erica had changed into a pair of tight jeans that accented her small waist and long legs and topped it with a cropped navy blue shirt that left enough room at the bottom for Amanda to make out the small gold ring piercing her belly button. She'd washed off most of the makeup, and her hair was brushed and pulled back into a blue scrunchie.

"I said, what are you doing?"

Sister Carlson picked up the book and brushed off the dirt so that the gold lettering shone in the darkened room. "You have a Book of Mormon."

"Yeah. So what? I didn't steal it. These two guys gave it to me a long time ago."

"Missionaries?" Amanda asked.

"Yeah, I guess."

"Have you read it?" continued Sister Carlson.

"Some. Who did you say you were again?"

"We're also missionaries from The Church of Jesus Christ of Latter-day Saints, and we have been sent from Heavenly Father to talk to you today." Sister Carlson sat down on the couch.

Amanda followed her companion's example. The whole visit felt surreal.

Erica remained standing. "Look, you got the wrong idea. I don't know why I called for that"—she stopped as if biting off a swear word—"that bible. And I don't know why I never threw away that Mormon book either. But you gotta see that I ain't the churchy type. So maybe you two should just go."

"Do you like books?" asked Amanda, trying to change the subject a little and lighten the tension that had developed.

"Don't I look like I can read?" She narrowed her eyes and stared coldly at the sisters.

Ignoring the question, Amanda continued. "What kind of books do you like?"

For some reason, the question made Erica laugh, and she sat down on a kitchen chair. "The thing is that I don't have too much free time for reading. If you know what I mean."

Before Amanda could reply, her companion jumped in. "Do you mind if we start with a prayer?"

Erica leaned forward. "Well, I don't think—" she began.

"And if you don't mind," continued Sister Carlson, her arms already folded and her head bowed, "I'll just go ahead and say it."

After the prayer, the sisters began the lesson. At first Erica looked edgy and uncomfortable, but as the time passed, she seemed to become genuinely interested in what the sisters were teaching her. She had lots of questions, and twice she asked them to repeat a concept.

"You know," began Erica, "I figured you would start preaching how God was gonna send me to hell. But you're telling me I'm His child and that He loves me? Are you sure you're a real religion 'cause it don't sound like no religion I ever heard of."

"Why would you be going to hell?" Amanda asked.

Sister Carlson turned to her companion, disbelief written all over her face.

"There are people who think that there will be more work for hookers in hell than in heaven," Erica said with a grin.

Amanda felt a sudden rush of heat to her face. "You're a hooker?" she said without thinking.

The words barely left Amanda's mouth before Erica had begun to laugh again. It was a warm, contagious sound, and soon both sisters were laughing with her.

"What did you think?" Erica wiped her eye with one hand and picked the handcuffs up off the table with the other. "That I worked in a bank or something?"

Amanda shook her head. "I guess I thought you were in security."

That sent them into another spasm of laughter.

When things finally calmed down, Amanda turned to Erica. "This may be totally inappropriate, and if it is, I hope you'll forgive me, but how did you become a . . . ?"

"A prostitute?" Erica shrugged. "I guess it was either this, deal drugs, or starve. You don't plan on it or nothing; you're just trying to get by. But some day I'm gonna get out. Maybe learn to cut hair or something."

Amanda searched the young woman's face. She couldn't even imagine what it was like to live that way. "Don't you have family or someone who could help you?"

She shook her head. "No. It was just my mom and me, but now she's gone."

"I'm sorry," Sister Carlson said.

"No, don't be. You think any mother'd be proud to have a daughter who's a hooker?"

"Well, aren't there places where you can go?" Amanda pushed on. "Organizations that would help—"

"Look, I don't need to be saved or nothing," Erica interrupted. "I do what I gotta do. I'm just saying that someday it's gonna be different. That's all."

Amanda had no idea how to respond. For a few moments no one spoke.

Finally Sister Carlson broke the silence. "We'd like to keep teaching you, Erica. Is that okay?"

She pushed a loose strand of hair out of her eyes. "Yeah, that'd be good."

Amanda felt the Spirit burning within her. "Heavenly Father loves you more than you can even imagine, but He wants you to have the freedom to make your own choices. We make choices every day, and some bring us happiness and joy while others bring us sorrow. But it's that freedom to choose and what we do with it that's the greatest evidence we can have our Father's love."

Erica looked thoughtfully at the two sister missionaries.

As the sisters drove home, Amanda found herself remembering the things Elder Castro had said the day before at the district activity, and it made her grin. She couldn't wait to tell him about this.

Chapter Eleven

April 24, 2009

Dear Jake,

I need to hear from you. It's been almost two months and I'm getting really anxious. Are you having trouble with school? Are you sick? I just don't understand why you haven't written. Please get back to me soon. I miss you so much, and it's worse when I don't hear from you.

Love always,
Amanda

"I DON'T LIKE THAT ONE. He's mean."

Amanda was balancing little Joshua on her knee with one hand and holding the book open in front of them with the other. She'd brought over the children's illustrated Book of Mormon, and she was showing Josh the pictures.

"He does look mean," agreed Amanda. "His name is Laban, and he wants to kill Nephi and his brothers."

"That's bad." Joshua reached out and turned the page.

While Amanda entertained the little boy, her companion was talking with his mother. They'd discovered early on that Kitiara could get more out of the lessons if one of the sisters kept her toddler busy.

Holding the small child in her arms with his curly hair brushing against her chin, Amanda found herself wondering what it would be like to have a child of her own. Perhaps someday there would be a little boy with Jake's red hair and her blue-green eyes. She would teach him to love music and books right from the very start.

"The end," Joshua said, grabbing the back cover of the book and closing it with a smack. He slid off her lap so quickly she dropped the book on the floor.

"Stay there," he commanded before running in the direction of his room.

But as the thought of Jake came to her mind, a sense of uneasiness followed. It had been weeks since his last letter. Amanda knew he was busy with school and his activities in the singles ward. Still, how much time could it take to drop her a note and say hi?

"Look."

Her thoughts were interrupted as a bright green dump truck was pushed up into her face.

"Now, Joshy, you be nice," said his mother, looking over at him from the couch. "We don't push things in people's faces."

Joshua stuck his thumb in his mouth and looked down at the ground as the toy hung from his hand in dejection.

"He's okay," Amanda assured his mother as she pulled Joshua back up on her lap. "What a beautiful truck."

"He really likes you," Kitiara said.

Amanda jostled the child up and down on her knee. "And I like him."

Sister Carlson had her planner open on her lap and was flipping through the pages. "Let's find a date for your baptism."

They'd been teaching Kitiara for nearly a month now, and she'd been to church several Sundays in a row. Earlier in the week, the sisters had presented the baptismal challenge, and Kitiara had promised to pray about it. Upon their return today, she'd announced her decision to become a member as soon as possible.

They decided that the baptism would take place two weeks from the following Sunday and that Kitiara's interview with the district leader would be held the afternoon before. Joshua stood at the door as the sisters left, waving his little hand until they drove away.

"This is exciting," Sister Carlson said, braking at a stoplight. "I think we should celebrate."

"What did you have in mind?"

"A double-fudge chocolate shake and some cheese fries from Squeezy's."

Amanda laughed. "In other words, a fattening celebration."

"Is there any other kind?"

Twenty minutes later, they sat across from one another on a picnic bench in front of the tiny shop. They'd split the milkshake into two cups and were sharing a basket of cheese fries.

Sister Carlson took a long sip from her straw. "This is so good. I don't even care if it's loaded with sugars, trans fats, and lots of other horrible things. It tastes heavenly."

Amanda nibbled on a french fry. The sky was clear, and the April sun felt warm on her back, making her feel a little sleepy.

"We'll have to call the DL as soon as we get home and set up Kitiara's interview," Sister Carlson said. "I hope everything goes okay over the next couple of weeks."

"What do you mean?" Amanda asked.

Sister Carlson finished the last of her shake and then tossed her cup into a nearby garbage can. "In the past, it seems that just before a baptism, something bad often happens. It's as if Satan is challenging our investigators right up to the last minute."

"But what could possibly go wrong?"

"Hopefully nothing. Still, let's make sure we pray extra hard for her this week."

A sudden chill ran up Amanda's spine, and she pulled her sweater closer before standing up.

* * *

Looking back over the days that followed, Amanda wondered if that chill might have been a warning of things to come, a reflection of the spiritual and emotional roller-coaster ride that awaited her.

At nine-fifteen on the morning of their next lesson the sister missionaries arrived at Erica's building. They'd been teaching her for nearly three weeks now, and she'd been progressing well. Sister Carlson was hoping to convince her to come to church with them the following Sunday.

As they walked down the poorly lit hallway outside Erica's apartment, the door flew open and a middle-aged man, his shirt open and his hair rumpled, charged out. The strong smell of alcohol preceded him as he pushed past the sisters and stumbled to the stairs.

"Don't you ever come back here," screamed Erica from the door. She followed the command with a string of vulgar words that made Amanda squirm.

"Sorry, Sisters," Erica said without looking at them. "Welcome to my world."

The black filmy wrap Erica had thrown around her shoulders did little to cover the lacy red bra and panties underneath. One strap had slipped down her arm. Her long hair had fallen across her face, and when she reached up to push it back, Amanda could see a welt around her wrist.

"You're hurt," Sister Carlson said, pointing to the wound, but the girl quickly pulled her arm away and turned back into the apartment.

"Occupational hazard," she said over her shoulder. Her voice was cool. "He put the cuffs on too tight."

Amanda knew that Erica had been honest about her profession right from the start, but whenever the sisters were there, she was always dressed modestly and the apartment was spotlessly clean. As they taught Erica, she seemed to glow with an inner light. It was easy to forget that her life had an ugly side to it. The shock of seeing the two worlds collide left Amanda disconcerted.

The sisters entered the apartment and found Erica seated on the couch wrapped in a blanket.

"I'll get some ice," said Sister Carlson heading toward the kitchen past a pile of empty beer cans stacked together on the dining room table.

Amanda sat down next to the woman on the couch while Sister Carlson applied a dish towel full of ice to her wrist.

"Are you okay?" Sister Carlson asked. "Do you need to see a doctor?"

"Just go. Get out of here."

"Tell us what happened."

"What happened?" Erica shook her head in disbelief. "I'm a hooker. I have sex with men for money, and some of them like it rough. This time it got a little out of control. That's all." Her voice had risen to an almost hysterical pitch.

She stood up, the blanket slipping from her shoulders as she folded her arms across her chest. "This is my life, and it ain't gonna change. All that stuff about Jesus and repentance. It doesn't work here. Just leave now!"

Amanda shrunk back at the onslaught. The girl was embarrassed and hurting, that was obvious.

"We'll go." Sister Carlson stood, gathering her books. "But before we do, I want you to know that you are a child of God and that He loves you, and with His help, you can overcome anything."

In response, Erica walked to the door and pulled it open.

Amanda got up as well, but before leaving, she reached into her purse and pulled out a small card. "This has the mission address and phone number on it. If you ever need anything . . ." She held it out, but the other woman refused to take it. Instead, Amanda left it on the small table, the one where they'd first seen the dusty Book of Mormon.

The door slammed behind them, and Amanda could hear Erica's sobs coming through the thin wood. For a moment both sisters stood in the hall staring at one another. Amanda felt so helpless.

"There's nothing more we can do here," Sister Carlson said. "Let's go."

* * *

Losing Erica was a deep disappointment to both sisters, but especially to Amanda. They discussed going back again, but Sister Carlson said she had a strong prompting that for the time being they needed to give her some room. However, the loss was tempered with the joy of Kitiara's upcoming baptism.

It was a beautiful California morning as the sisters drove to the stake center to meet Kitiara and the elders for her baptismal interview. Amanda gazed out the window as they drove. The surrounding hills, usually cloaked in golden brown grass, were now green from the recent spring rains, and multicolored wildflowers had popped up along the side of the road.

Over the past two weeks, Amanda had been wondering whether Kitiara and Joshua could be the family from her dream. They certainly seemed to meet the criteria. Especially once the mother and son were able to be sealed in the temple to her husband.

And yet Amanda was still unsure. If this was the family she'd been sent to find, wouldn't there be a sense of peace or of a job accomplished? Something that would assure her that the dream was now fulfilled? But when she prayed about it, Amanda couldn't feel the reassurance she sought.

The elders were already in the church building when the sisters arrived. Elder Castro was using the phone in the hall, and Elder Hoyle sat on a nearby chair flipping through his scriptures.

"Find any new commandments we don't know about?" quipped Sister Carlson, settling herself onto the couch across from him.

The elder looked up in surprise. "Excuse me?"

"She was just being cute," Amanda assured him as she sat down next to her companion.

Sister Carlson chuckled. "Did anyone ever tell you that you take all the fun out of a joke, Sister Kelly?"

Before Amanda could reply, Elder Castro, who had finished his phone call, joined the group.

"We were in the office this morning," he said, "and the APs asked us to drop off the mail. Save them a couple of bucks forwarding it out to our apartments."

"That was nice of you," Amanda responded as she took her letters and began flipping through them.

"Well, you know us—nicest elders in the mission," said Elder Castro, laughing. "By the way, Sister Carlson, I was wondering if you could help me out with something. I've been asked to sing "A Poor Wayfaring Man of Grief" in priesthood this week. Elder Van said he thought you played the piano."

Amanda looked up in surprise. She and Sister Carlson had been companions for almost two months, and never once had she mentioned her interest in music. "Is that true?" Amanda asked.

"Depends on your definition of the word *play*."

"Well, I'm desperate, and I need to practice with a piano," Elder Castro said. "Could you please run through it with me a couple of times before your investigator gets here? We could use the piano in the chapel."

Sister Carlson looked at her companion.

"Go ahead," Amanda said. "Just leave the door open, and I'll get you as soon as Kitiara arrives."

Once her companion had left, Amanda sat down, eager to read her mail. One letter in particular caught her eye. The handwriting was achingly familiar. She hadn't heard from Jake for more than two months.

She opened the envelope with anticipation.

As she read, her eagerness was replaced by a sickening knot in her stomach. He didn't actually start out with "Dear Jane," but Amanda didn't have to go very far to get the gist.

April 26, 2009

Dear Amanda,

This is the hardest letter I've ever had to write. I wish there was some way we could talk in person, but since you're on a mission, I have no other option. I guess the best thing is to just say it. I'm getting married in June to a really wonderful girl. Her name is Diane, she's a freshman at BYU, and she lives in my apartment complex. In fact, she's in my family home evening group, believe it or not. I wasn't looking for anyone, but it just happened.

I can't tell you how awful I feel, but really I'm sure this is for the best. If I could fall in love with someone else, then evidently you and I were not meant to be. And I know that there will be some great guy out there for you too. I hope that we can always stay friends.

Best wishes,

Jake

She'd never even suspected there was someone else in his life.

The sound of piano chords accompanying a somewhat shaky tenor voice drifted to her ears, but Amanda's thoughts had traveled back to the night before she'd entered the MTC.

She and Jake had sat on the front steps of her house and talked until nearly two in the morning. Then Jake had taken her in his arms and held her close. The stubble on his chin had tickled her as he softly kissed her.

"I'll wait for you," he promised, his mouth pressed against her ear. "Just like you waited for me."

Yeah, right, Amanda thought. *You couldn't even make it through a lousy nine months.*

She looked up to find the young elder across the room watching her. What had he seen in her face, she wondered. Could he tell that the only man she had ever loved had just dumped her for some nineteen-year-old husband hunter? Amanda searched for something to say that would ease the discomfort she was feeling.

"Do you sing?" she asked.

"Nope," he replied. "At least not the kind of singing that anyone would want to listen to."

"Me neither, but I do play the French horn."

"Oh," he said, nodding politely.

All the hurt Amanda was feeling searched for an outlet, and as she looked at Elder Hoyle, her anger boiled over. How dare he just sit there watching her like she was a TV program? He must have seen the pain on her face. Any decent human being would have turned away, given her a little privacy.

"My brother plays the oboe. That's in the same family as a French horn, isn't it?" he added.

"The oboe is a woodwind, and the French horn is a brass instrument. But don't worry. Most people don't know the difference." She spoke as if she was addressing a five-year-old.

Elder Hoyle hadn't missed the patronizing tone, and he looked confused. "Oh, I see."

"So you're into sports, I bet," Amanda continued. "A real athletic type. A jock."

Elder Hoyle's neck began to turn red, and his voice became defensive. "I like to play sports, I guess, but I'm not a jock."

"Oh, really? So you're telling me that you're some math genius or maybe a rocket scientist?"

"I didn't say that." The color had moved up his neck and was now sweeping up his face.

Amanda glanced at the door to the parking lot. Now would be a really good time for Kitiara to show up. "You guys are all alike," she said bitterly.

"I don't know what your problem is," he said, flipping open his scriptures and turning away from her.

Amanda got up and walked toward the door. What was she doing? She hadn't behaved that way since she was nine. Elder Hoyle must think she was out of her mind. *Perhaps I should say something, maybe apologize,* she thought, sneaking a quick glance in the elders' direction. But Elder Hoyle had his back turned to her, and Amanda didn't have the nerve to try.

She turned toward the door, trying to distract herself from the ache that threatened to consume her, and forced her thoughts to Kitiara. Where was she?

"I'm going to try her cell phone," Amanda said to no one in particular as she opened her purse and pulled out her planner.

The phone rang three times before it was answered. When Kitiara finally did speak, her voice was barely audible against the clamor of a siren. Amanda covered her free ear and spoke loudly. "This is Sister Kelly. Is everything okay?"

With all the noise, it was difficult for Amanda to hear. Once she did make out what Kitiara was saying, she yelled into the phone, "We'll be there soon." Sister Carlson returned to the lobby with Elder Castro just as she hung up.

"What happened?" Elder Castro asked.

"There was some kind of accident, I think. Kitiara and Josh are at the hospital. I told her we'd come right away."

"We'll go with you," he said. "If someone is hurt they might need a priesthood blessing."

"Good idea." Sister Carlson pulled the keys from her purse. "You can follow us."

Chapter Twelve

THE LOBBY OF THE EMERGENCY room was crowded as Amanda and her companion made their way to the front desk. The elders followed them in and remained by the front door.

Two women in matching blue sweaters oversaw the reception area. One was talking on the phone, and the other was attempting to calm a distraught older woman.

Amanda took several deep breaths, trying to control her panic as she waited her turn to be helped.

"What can I do for you?" The woman on the phone had finished her call and was now addressing the sisters.

Amanda cleared her throat. "Kitiara Williams and her son, Joshua, were just brought here by ambulance and we wanted to see them."

The woman turned to a computer at her right and began typing. "Are you family?" she asked.

"No," answered Sister Carlson. "We're good friends."

The woman looked up from the monitor. "I'm sorry, but I am not allowed to give out patient information without their consent."

Amanda's stress was high, and it came across in her tone of voice. "Couldn't someone go ask her?"

"I'm sorry, but we're very busy today. You can have a seat and wait if you wish."

Amanda turned to her companion. "What are we going to do?" she asked.

"I don't think we have much choice. We'll have to wait."

Ten minutes dragged by before Kitiara came out. Her hair was disheveled, and she had a huge greenish bruise on the left side of her face.

The sisters stood up and made their way through the crowd to her side. As soon as she saw them, a look of relief passed over the woman's features. "You're here."

Amanda hugged her tightly. "Are you all right?"

"A few bruises, that's all. A car ran a red light and plowed right into us." Her face began to crumple, and tears came to her eyes. "But they think one of Josh's kidneys was damaged. He may need to have surgery."

"The elders came with us," Sister Carlson said, waving them over. "They can give him a blessing if you'd like."

"That would be so good." Kitiara sighed.

The four missionaries followed Kitiara to the examining room where the toddler lay in a large metal crib. He had IVs hooked up to his arms and a plastic mask covering his nose and mouth. His dark eyes were open, and he looked frightened and confused. He whimpered softly.

"It's okay, baby, Mommy's here." Kitiara moved closer to the bed so she could reach in and hold his hand. "They did some tests, and the doctor is supposed to be back with the results soon."

He looked so small and scared. Amanda felt a sob collecting in her throat. For a moment she couldn't breathe, but she fought the emotion welling inside her. She had to be strong.

The elders moved to the other side of the bed and prepared to give Josh a blessing. Elder Hoyle anointed, the drop of oil disappearing quickly into the mass of dark curls. "What's his full name?" he asked.

"Joshua David Williams," whispered Kitiara.

Once the anointing was completed, Elder Castro and Elder Hoyle placed their hands lightly on the child's head and proceeded to bless him. Amanda listened intently, waiting for words that would assure her the boy would be healed. But they didn't come. Comfort and strength were promised, but not healing.

A cold hand seemed to grip her heart as the amens were said. What did it mean? Was the Lord going to take this baby just like he'd taken his father?

The door opened, and a heavyset Latina nurse walked in. "What do you think this is?" she demanded, placing her hands on her hips. "A party? The sign says no more than two visitors at a time. Some of you will have to leave."

Kitiara began to cry. "Couldn't the two sister missionaries stay with me? I don't have anyone else."

The nurse's eyes softened. "I'm not supposed to, but I guess it would be all right just this once. But for Pete's sake, keep it down. I don't want any of the other patients on the floor thinking they can do it too."

Amanda smiled gratefully. "Thank you."

Once the nurse had shooed the elders out of the room, she returned with a clipboard. Amanda watched anxiously as she checked Joshua's vitals and noted them on his chart.

A few minutes later a short, balding Arabic doctor entered the room. He reviewed the chart and then stood at the foot of the bed, his arms crossed as he contemplated the small patient before him. At last he turned to Kitiara.

"It looks like he may have suffered some damage to his left kidney, but at this point we are unsure of the degree of his injuries. I think we should send him into surgery right away. We'll know more once we get in there."

Kitiara gasped, and Amanda wrapped her arms around the woman's shoulders.

"As with any surgery, there are risks," the doctor continued. "Especially for a child this young. But until we know the extent of the damage, I feel this is the only viable option we have."

Kitiara pushed her hair back from her face. "When will you operate?"

"As soon as we can have him prepped."

Amanda exchanged a worried look with her companion. If anything were to happen to Josh, it would destroy his mother.

The doctor signed the chart and then handed it back to the nurse who stood waiting at his side. "The anesthesiologist and his team will be here momentarily."

"Can I stay with him?" Kitiara asked.

"It's best if you leave now. Someone will show you to the surgery waiting room. I'll come out to you as soon as the surgery is over."

The nurse lowered the side of the crib, and Kitiara, who was crying again, bent over her son and kissed him softly on the forehead. "It'll be okay, big guy. Momma loves you. I'll be right here when you wake up."

He reached his hands out imploringly and whispered, "Momma," as they left. It was all Amanda could do to keep her own emotions under control.

The waiting room was empty except for Kitiara and the four missionaries. It was nearly six in the evening, and all the regularly scheduled operations had been over long before. The nurse had told them that the surgery was expected to last two or three hours.

Amanda had been pacing the floor for the last thirty minutes, and her legs were as tired as her emotions. The clock on the wall seemed to move with agonizing slowness.

Sinking onto a hard plastic chair, Amanda looked around the room. Sister Carlson and Kitiara sat in one corner talking quietly. Elder Castro had his journal out and was writing in it, and Elder Hoyle stood staring out the window. The light from the setting sun silhouetted his body and brought out the reddish highlights in his hair.

It had been such a long day. First the shock of Jake's letter, then the scene between her and Elder Hoyle, and now Josh. Amanda rested her forehead on her upturned palms. *Oh, please, Heavenly Father,* she prayed. *Let him be okay.*

As she bent forward in her seat, Amanda could feel the corners of the letter press against her body. She'd hastily shoved it in her pocket earlier that afternoon, right after she'd finished reading it. She didn't want to take it out now, didn't want to read the words again.

A heavy feeling settled over her heart. Just knowing he was at home, loving her and waiting, had given Amanda comfort and strength when she was down, and when she hadn't heard from him these past months, it had made her feel empty. Now, sitting in the darkening hospital waiting room alone with the pain of Jake's rejection, Amanda felt as if she'd paid too heavy a price to follow her dream, and she couldn't help wondering if it had been worth it.

If I was home, Jake and I would be married now, and I might have even been pregnant with my own baby.

Amanda's hand drifted down to her waist as if trying to feel the life that could have been growing inside her. She'd loved and trusted Jake so much. How could he have done this to her?

Elder Hoyle turned from the window and came toward her. He sat down in the chair next to Amanda's, and she looked up.

"I want to apologize about this afternoon," he said. "I don't know what I did to upset you, but I didn't mean it."

Amanda looked at him in amazement. Everything had been her fault. He must realize that. Yet he was willing to take responsibility in order to resolve things.

"It wasn't you. It was me," she said. "I received some painful news, and I guess I took it out on you. It's no excuse, I know, but I'm sorry."

He smiled at her and his eyes crinkled a little at the side. "No harm done."

They sat for a moment in silence and then Amanda turned to him. "Can I ask you something?"

"Sure."

"When you and Elder Castro gave that blessing to Joshua, why didn't it say he would be healed?"

Elder Hoyle shifted slightly in his seat. "Hmm . . . I can't answer for Elder Castro, and, of course, he was the voice. But I can tell you what I felt."

Amanda bent forward.

"As the words were spoken I felt very sure that the blessing was inspired by Heavenly Father."

"So are you saying that God didn't want Joshua healed?" Amanda asked.

"I didn't say that." Elder Hoyle ran his fingers through his hair. "I haven't given very many blessings, but I think sometimes Heavenly Father wants us to use our own faith, to trust Him without everything being fully explained. I don't know what will happen to Joshua, but I'm confident that Heavenly Father does, and if we put our trust in Him, then we don't have to worry."

Amanda considered his words. "It's hard, though. Especially when things happen that don't seem fair or right." She was thinking about Jake again. Had it been wrong of her to come on a mission instead of getting married? She'd been so sure that her decision to go had been the right one.

"It is hard, I know," Elder Hoyle agreed. "But if we trust Heavenly Father—really put our faith in His hands—then we can have confidence that He has a plan for us. Heavenly Father loves us and wants us to grow and be happy."

His words brought the warmth of the Spirit. She thought about the family from her dream and the other people she'd taught so far. Then she considered the many lessons and spiritual truths she'd learned herself while serving on this mission. A feeling of love and heavenly acceptance washed over Amanda, supplanting some of the pain.

She looked up at Elder Hoyle and found that he was watching her closely. Yet this time, she understood that it was a sign of his concern for her. It made her happy to know that he cared enough to be interested in how she felt. It was sweet, really.

For a moment, as their eyes joined, time seemed to stand still, and it felt as if he could actually feel the joy that she felt.

"Mrs. Williams?" The doctor had come into the waiting room. He looked tired but there was a smile on his face.

Kitiara stood and hurried toward him. "Is Josh okay?"

"He's fine," the doctor said. "And he's resting comfortably in recovery."

"Praise the Lord," Kitiara said in relief.

"There was some minor damage to the kidney and some internal bruising, but we were able to repair it. He should be up and running around in a few weeks."

"Thank you, thank you!" Kitiara cried, pumping the doctor's hand up and down. "Thank you for saving my baby."

"The nurse will take you to the pediatrics department. He should be up in about thirty minutes."

Sister Carlson glanced at her watch. "It's getting late," she said. "We were supposed to be at an appointment a half an hour ago."

"Give Joshua a kiss for us," Amanda said, sliding her purse strap over her shoulder. "We'll call you tomorrow."

The elders gathered their things together as well in preparation to go, and Amanda turned to join her companion.

She turned her thoughts to the letter still resting in her pocket. She pulled it out, crumpled it in her fist, and tossed it into a garbage can. Losing Jake had hurt, and she would grieve the loss for a long time. But being a missionary had changed her life. The opportunity to serve people like Kitiara and her son was the best thing she'd ever done. No one knew what the future would bring, least of all Amanda, but for tonight at least, she could turn it over to Heavenly Father.

Chapter Thirteen

It was well into May when Amanda stood next to the font with Josh holding her hand as she watched Kitiara get baptized. Her dark face, set off by the white of the baptismal jumpsuit, glowed with joy. It wasn't hard for Amanda to imagine her dressed in temple white and being sealed to her husband and baby sometime next year.

Someone took a picture of Kitiara before her baptism, surrounded by her son and the sisters, and gave Amanda a copy. She stuck it in her mission journal as a treasured memento.

There was a good turnout by the ward as well, and there must have been something about the spirit of the baptism, because the following week the sisters received missionary referrals from two ward members.

Erica, their prostitute investigator, had packed up her bags one day and disappeared. When they tried to visit her, the landlord told them that she'd paid up her rent and moved on without leaving a message or a forwarding address. Amanda could only hope that her beloved friend would be safe and continue to study that Book of Mormon so that one day she might be ready to accept the Savior's atoning blood.

At the end of the month, Amanda was saddened to receive word that she was being transferred. When it came time to leave, both she and Sister Carlson had tears in their eyes and promised to keep in touch and to get together after their missions. Like her first area, Santa Clara had become a special place to Amanda, and she found it just as hard to move on as it had been on her first transfer.

* * *

The next five months passed quickly, and before she knew it, Amanda had been serving in California for fifteen months. While October in Utah often meant snow flurries and cold temperatures, here in Saratoga, it was still warm enough to tract in just a light jacket. Her companion didn't even need that.

"You don't know cold till you've lived through sixty-seven Minnesota winters," Sister Prichert said with a big grin.

They'd been companions for nearly three months now, and any preconceived ideas Amanda had had concerning senior sister missionaries disappeared completely the day she met Sister Prichert.

"Now, just because I'm older, it doesn't mean I'm your mother or your grandmother. I don't pick up other people's junk. I only make my bed. I take turns at cooking, and I haven't found a young sister I couldn't keep up with. Any questions?"

"I don't think so." Amanda tried hard to keep a straight face.

True to her word, Sister Prichert had proved to be hardworking. Other than taking a daily pill for her blood pressure, she was in excellent health and full of energy and enthusiasm.

That afternoon the sisters had chosen to tract a subdivision of small, well-kept, boxy homes. They'd been at it for a couple of hours but hadn't had any luck.

Turning a corner, they found themselves approaching a shabby, run-down dwelling. The structure was badly in need of paint, and the yard was covered with brown, scrubby patches of grass. A beat-up Camero balanced precariously on a set of jacks in the driveway, and the front porch awning sagged heavily in the middle.

"Your turn," Sister Prichert said, stepping back and allowing Amanda to take the lead up the walkway.

They'd only gone a few steps when a huge black dog appeared behind the flimsy screen door, barking ferociously and pressing against the mesh barrier. Amanda froze in place. "I think maybe we'd better pass on this house," she said, cautiously eyeing the vicious canine.

"Nonsense." Her companion pushed past her. "I know dogs. He's all bark and no bite. Come on."

Amanda hesitated a moment before joining the older woman, who was already knocking sharply on the wooden frame.

A huge hand yanked the dog back, and in its place stood its equally ferocious-looking owner. *This isn't a man,* thought Amanda looking up at the towering figure before her. His wifebeater was embellished with the logo from a popular beer company and exposed massive biceps covered with colorful tattoos. *I think we've discovered the missing link.*

"What?" he growled.

"We're missionaries from The . . ." began Sister Prichert.

"Look, I don't care what you're selling. I'm not interested. Get off my property!" he said, including a few colorful expletives.

Amanda began to back off, but her companion didn't move.

"Excuse me?" Sister Prichert said.

"Do you want me to come out and kick your—"

"We're going now." Amanda grabbed her companion by the arm and dragged her down the steps toward the street.

An unexpected splash of cold water made Amanda spin around quickly. The sprinklers had just been turned on, and the man stood next to the water spigot, chuckling, before he returned to the darkness of his house.

Sister Prichert was so angry she couldn't even complete a sentence. "I have never, in all my time in this area, been treated in—who does that guy think he is, behaving in such a—well, I'm not just going to walk away and pretend . . ." She turned suddenly and marched through the sprinklers back to the house.

"Sister, stop!" yelled Amanda, but it was too late. Sister Prichert was already on the porch, knocking on the front door.

"You again!" sneered the man as he stepped into the doorway. "I thought I told you—"

"I have no doubt that you have a mother and a grandmother." *Sister Prichert sounds severe,* Amanda thought with an inward smile, like a strict schoolteacher. "And I am sure they would be horrified if they knew you had treated another elderly woman in such a disgraceful manner."

Amanda held her breath. Any minute she expected him to charge out, his fists swinging.

"What?" he began, but Sister Prichert didn't even take a breath.

"We are representatives of Jesus Christ and are here on His business. You should be ashamed of yourself."

His mouth hung open and his eyes glazed over.

"Take this." Sister Prichert pushed a pass-along card around the screen door. "And call the phone number on the back. They'll send you a book that I think you'll find very interesting."

He took the card without saying a word.

"Good. We are going to leave now, so will you please turn off the sprinklers?"

"Yes, ma'am," he responded, obviously cowed.

"Have a nice day," she said before walking down the steps and heading back to the sidewalk.

Amanda followed in amazement. Once they were out of earshot, she turned to her companion. "How did you do that?"

"Age has its benefits, you know," Sister Prichert said with a mischievous twinkle in her eye.

* * *

A cool wind blew down the street, and Amanda pulled her jacket a little closer. "I bet I've spent nearly a third of my mission tracting."

"I know what you mean," Sister Prichert said. "I wish we could teach even half as much. Still, we do get to meet some interesting people this way."

Amanda laughed. "That's true."

"Do you know that I tracted into some little people one time?" continued Sister Prichert. "The nicest family you'd ever want to meet."

Amanda laughed. "Well, I've never met any little people, but I actually taught a prostitute once."

"Prostitute? You're kidding."

"No, it's true. Her name was Erica. She was so bright, but she disappeared."

"Well, it keeps life exciting, doesn't it?" Sister Prichert slowed as they reached the corner at the end of the block. "You know, I don't think we have the right address. We've been all through this subdivision and I can't find a 343 on any street."

For the last two hours, they'd been searching for a less-active member whose records had just been transferred into the ward. At the same time they'd tracted out a few houses as well.

Amanda nodded. "We've probably walked by it a dozen times without knowing. Well, I guess we can recheck with the ward clerk next Sunday."

As they returned to their car, Amanda felt a nagging sensation, like she'd forgotten something. She slipped her hand into the pocket of her jacket to reassure herself that the car keys were still there. Everything seemed fine, but the unsettled feeling persisted.

"Do you remember if we knocked on the door of that house over there?" Amanda pointed to a two-story green stucco on the corner across the street.

"Wasn't that where the woman threatened to let her Chihuahua attack us?"

"That's right." Amanda vaguely remembered a grumpy lady and a small yippy dog. They'd knocked on so many doors today that it was difficult to keep them straight. "I just keep thinking there's something we're forgetting."

Sister Prichert shook her head. "I don't have anything scheduled on the planner."

"Never mind. It's probably nothing. Let's get going."

The streets in the neighborhood circled around each other in a serpentine pattern, and the sisters had to double back in order to reach the main road. For the second time that day, they found themselves in front of the green stucco home, and Amanda felt an intense stirring within.

"I know this is crazy, but I think we should try that house again," she said, pulling over to the curb.

"Okay with me. Besides, what's the worst a little Chihuahua like that could do? Steal our shoes?"

They made their way to the entrance, passing through a courtyard lined with large clay pots full of flowering vines. Most of the plants were dying, but a few hardy varieties still displayed their blooms. An ornate brass crucifix with the figure of Jesus hanging in agony decorated the front door.

The sisters exchanged glances. Most of the Catholic families in this area were Latino, and since neither sister spoke a word of Spanish, communication could be difficult.

Amanda knocked on the door, and the sisters waited expectantly for the sound of high-pitched barking. Instead, they heard footsteps coming toward them. The lock was undone, the knob turned, and the door opened slightly to reveal the face of a young woman peering shyly out at them. Her bronze skin and beautiful dark hair suggested her Latin American heritage.

"Hello," Amanda said, waiting to hear a string of Spanish words.

"Hello," she responded, and Amanda breathed a sigh of relief. The young woman spoke English.

"I'm Sister Kelly and this is Sister Prichert. We have a message about Jesus Christ that we would like to share with you today. Would you have a few minutes to listen?"

She didn't answer at first.

"Do you speak English?" Amanda asked, her spirits sinking.

The young woman looked up and gave them an unexpected smile. "Yes," she said, her golden-brown eyes sparkling. "Come." She opened the door and motioned them to enter.

The home was Spanish in decor, with heavy wood furniture upholstered in thick red-and-gold velvet fabrics. Cumbersome drapes were pulled shut across the windows, giving everything a dark and gloomy appearance.

The sisters followed the young woman through the house to a small sunroom behind the kitchen where light poured in through the windows on every side. She sat down and motioned for the sisters to do the same.

"I like this room," she said softly.

"I can see why," Sister Prichert said. "It's airy and bright."

The young woman had a strong Spanish accent that sounded different to Amanda than the Mexican accents she often heard. She wondered if the girl might be from Puerto Rico or Cuba.

"My name is Noelia Mora. Please tell to me your message."

Amanda smiled. It usually took a bit of small talk before the missionaries could begin teaching, but this young lady was anxious to get down to business.

"Heavenly Father has a plan for each of His children on the earth," Amanda began. Noelia listened with great interest, and they taught her for over an hour.

Noelia's questions demonstrated a quick mind and a full understanding of what the sister missionaries taught. Amanda hadn't seen an investigator so eager to learn in a long time. When Sister Prichert produced a Book of Mormon in Spanish, Noelia promised to read it that very day.

"Can we come back Saturday and talk more?" Amanda asked eagerly.

A shadow passed over the girl's features. "No, tomorrow no is good. My *tia* is here tomorrow."

"Tia?" asked Sister Prichert.

"Tia, it means . . . how do you say . . . aunt."

"We could teach her as well," Amanda suggested. She was already imagining a whole family like Noelia, hungering and thirsting for the gospel.

"No, you not understand. My tia no is a good lady. She be very mad if she know I let you in her home and talk with you. Maybe you come again next week when she is no here."

Amanda felt a twinge of guilt. "We want to teach you, but we don't want to get you in trouble. Could we meet somewhere else?"

Noelia shook her head more firmly. "I cannot leave, only to do shopping." The girl appeared sincerely frightened by the thought of her tia's anger. "I have twenty-one years, and that is legal age here, no? I not need her permission to speak to you. If you come Tuesday, in the morning, then everything is good."

The time was set, and Noelia said good-bye, hugging them both.

* * *

The sound of fists pounding on the front door of the cheap resident motel had awakened Erica from a deep sleep.

Before she could get up, her pimp, Zack, smashed the door open, followed by an apelike bodyguard.

"Wait out here," Zack ordered the bodyguard before walking into the room. He stood next to the bed and surveyed Erica as if she were a piece of moldy beef. "Baby, you haven't been working for a while, and everyone's wonderin' why."

His voice was tender, almost gentle, but Erica knew better. Zack was a cold and dangerous man. She began to shake under the blankets.

"I'm not doing it no more," she said, her voice barely more than a whisper.

Over the last few months Erica had begun to feel disillusioned and depressed. It was becoming more difficult to service the men who used her body for their own needs, and listening to the sisters had only made it worse. She'd felt like she was being torn in two. She hoped that asking the sisters to leave would make the feelings go away. But it didn't help.

She'd tried moving in with a couple of other hookers, but that didn't work out either. Then two months ago, Erica had finally reached the breaking point, convinced that if she didn't quit while she could, she might never be able to get out. For nearly six weeks she'd managed to keep her whereabouts hidden from Zack and had begun to think she'd finally broken free.

"Erica, sweetheart, that's not how it goes. You work for me as long as I choose."

"No, Zack. I can't," she said, trying hard to control her fear.

He laughed. It was a low, ugly sound, and Erica shivered. He stuck his thumbs in his jean pockets, pushing the pants even lower down his hips than they already were. "By tomorrow I expect you back on the streets just like normal, and we'll forget this little incident ever happened."

Turning to the bodyguard as he passed the man in the hall, he said, "Make sure Miss Erica here remembers her commitments."

"No, please no!" begged Erica, pulling the blankets to her chest and pressing against the wall behind her. "I'll go back, I swear."

Even as the words left her lips, the bodyguard was already reaching for her. Before she could move away, he grabbed her by the arm and threw her across the room. A searing rush of pain blasted through her shoulder as she crashed against the wall. Before she could recover from the blow, he came at her again.

What followed was a cloudy blur, and Erica didn't want to remember. Afterwards all she could think about was getting away and fast. In desperation, she found herself heading to the only person in the world she trusted.

* * *

Amanda felt like she was floating as she and her companion drove onto the highway. "Noelia is a golden contact if I ever saw one."

"We never would have found her if you hadn't listened to that inspiration," added Sister Prichert. "Way to go."

A year before Amanda wouldn't have had the confidence to trust her spiritual feelings, but today she not only understood the Holy Ghost's prompting, she followed it as well. *I'm making progress.*

* * *

Erica left the dark interior of the bus and squinted in the afternoon glare of the Saratoga Greyhound Station. A beat-up looking café with filthy windows across the street apparently served as a waiting area for local taxi drivers. She fumbled in her handbag for her sunglasses, trying to ignore the aching in her arms and legs and the pain on the left side of her chest every time she moved.

Jerk. Probably cracked a rib, she thought as she waited for the sharpness of the agony to pass. *At least he didn't touch my face.*

She glanced around at the concrete building covered with colorful graffiti and sighed. All the cities in Silicon Valley pretty much looked the same. *I hope I'm doing the right thing,* she thought, pushing her hair back. *Not that I have any choice.* Sure, she could have gone to the cops, but when a pimp beats up one of his girls, the police weren't overly sympathetic.

She pulled a worn envelope from the pocket of her jeans and read the return address: *Sister Amanda Kelly, 2400 E. Rosemont Dr., Apt 3B, Saratoga, California.*

She'd had to come up with a pretty good story to get the sister missionaries' address. Erica had tried the mission office phone number first, but they'd refused to give the information out. Fortunately, she'd run into a couple of elders, and when she'd explained that Sister Kelly had left a valuable necklace at her apartment, the missionaries were happy to get her the information she needed. Erica felt awful about the lie, but considering her other sins, it was a relatively minor infraction.

The original idea had been to write her. Erica missed Sister Kelly's friendship, and she'd had some idea that maybe the young missionary might be the key to someday getting out of the racket. Little did Erica know then how desperately she would need Sister Kelly's help.

It took twenty minutes by cab and forty dollars she really couldn't afford to spend before she reached the apartment complex, only to find that the sisters were out. The ibuprofen that she'd been swallowing in large doses to keep the pain at a bearable level was beginning to wear off, and all she wanted was the oblivion of sleep. Erica tried to make herself comfortable on the top cement step while she waited for Sister Kelly to come home, but there was just no way. She hadn't thought about what she would say to Sister Kelly when she finally found her. It was enough just to be away from Zack and the life she'd left behind.

The sound of the sisters' voices drifted up from the landing below, and she caught her breath. In a few moments they would be on the stairs.

As Erica stood up, a wave of nausea nearly knocked her down. She grabbed the railing for support. "Sister Kelly?" The words sounded strange— as if someone else said them.

The sisters stopped at the bottom of the stairs, and Sister Kelly stared up in surprise.

Erica's vision began to blur as dizziness and confusion washed over her. She was vaguely aware that the older woman had moved toward her, and someone said, "I think she's going to faint," just before she passed out.

Chapter Fourteen

AMANDA, DRESSED IN HER PAJAMAS, sank gratefully onto her bed. It had been a very long day. Between the excitement of finding and teaching Noelia and then coming home to Erica collapsed on their doorstep, Amanda was emotionally exhausted.

Mission rules forbade guests staying in a missionary apartment, and Erica flatly refused to be taken to the emergency room. Sister Prichert had suggested they contact an older widowed sister in the ward. Emily Shumway had been happy to have Erica as a guest in her home, even scheduling an appointment with her own personal doctor when she realized the young woman was injured.

"Sister Shumway is a good person," Amanda said. "Taking in a total stranger without a question. I don't know if I would have done that."

"She is a good lady," her companion said from the bathroom, where she was putting her hair up in curlers for the night. "And I think she enjoyed the idea of having someone to look after."

Amanda lay back on her pillow and stared up at the ceiling. The sight of Erica had brought back memories of Santa Clara. Sister Carlson had written the week before and said that she was going home in about six weeks.

Sister Prichert had finished with her hair and began smearing white cold cream all over her face. "So tell me more about Erica. You taught her in the city, right?"

"Yes," Amanda said, rolling over on her side to look at her companion. "She was a media referral. She requested a Bible, and when we got to her apartment we actually found that she already had a Book of Mormon and had been reading it. The Spirit was so strong when we taught her, and I know she felt it."

"She was in a lot of pain today, but I can tell she's a sharp young lady."

"Oh, she is," agreed Amanda. "And that's what is really sad. I think that if things had been different she might have accepted the gospel."

"How do you mean?" Sister Prichert flipped off the bathroom light and sat on the bed.

"The problem is that Erica's . . . well, Erica's a prostitute," she said, expecting that this would fully explain the situation. But her companion stared at her blankly.

She tried again. "We tried to get her to change. We really did, but the lifestyle was just too deeply ingrained. Can you imagine what it would take for someone like that to transform their entire existence and join the Church? I'm not sure it would even be possible."

Sister Prichert's brow wrinkled, leaving little creases in the night cream. "That sounds rather judgmental, don't you think?"

Amanda felt as if she'd been slapped in the face. "I'm not judging her," she responded sharply. "I'm just stating the facts. She's a good person who's had an awful life. I'm happy to teach her but, realistically, where is it going to go?"

Sister Prichert frowned.

"Come on," Amanda said, feeling defensive, "how many prostitutes do you know of who have joined the Church?"

"None. But that's not the point." Sister Prichert leaned forward, staring intently at her companion. "Regardless of her past, she's still a daughter of Heavenly Father just like you and me, and we have no right to judge her potential."

Amanda resented the clear censure from her companion. *People don't change that much.* She tried to keep the sarcasm out of her voice as she replied, "You're right, I shouldn't judge, but I'm not holding my breath for her baptism either."

* * *

Noelia waited for the light under her aunt's door to go out before she slid the Book of Mormon from under her mattress. If she sat on the floor next to the window, she could read by the light of the street lamp. Noelia found the spot where she'd left off the night before and began reading. Soon, a warm, peaceful feeling filled her just as it had the last few nights. During the long hours of the day while she cooked and cleaned for her tia, Noelia had found herself longing for the moments she could steal away and read.

Growing up Catholic, she had attended mass every week and taken classes before her first communion. But in all that time, she'd never felt close to God. *La Virgin Maria* was different. She was beautiful and motherly. But *Dios,* the God that hung gaunt and tortured on the crucifix at the front of the church, had always been a frightening figure to her.

Yet here in the dark, as she read in 3 Nephi about Jesus and His love for mankind, Noelia felt a sense of joy and love she'd never known.

Early the next morning, Noelia met the sisters at the front door with a list of questions from her reading.

"So you finished 3 Nephi," Sister Kelly said. "That's great."

Noelia liked both sisters very much, but the young one with the beautiful long hair seemed familiar to her, as if they'd known one another before. "Si, and I read 1 Nephi, 2 Nephi, and Jacob too."

"My goodness," Sister Prichert said, "that's great! You could probably teach us now."

Noelia looked down. "*Pero* no. But please, I want to be baptized. What do I need to have baptism in this church?" The desire had entered her thoughts the night before, and now as she spoke the words, she could feel the Spirit confirming again that this was a righteous request.

Sister Kelly gazed at her as if surprised by the joy Noelia felt.

"I've never had someone ask to be baptized," Sister Prichert said. "And we definitely can arrange that, but first there are a few things we need to do."

Sister Kelly nodded. "We need to finish with the lessons, and you'll need to come to church for at least two Sundays."

"Oh," said Noelia, a sense of disappointment settling over her heart like a dark cloud.

"It won't be that long." Sister Kelly leaned forward. "A few weeks if you want."

Noelia shook her head as she considered the obstacles she would have to overcome. "I don't know if I can be baptized."

"Why not?" asked Sister Prichard.

Noelia couldn't look at the sisters. "You no understand," she said more firmly. "Not is possible for me go to church." It felt as if her world had suddenly crashed around her. How could these two American women understand the desperate situation she was in?

The younger sister leaned forward now, a look of real concern in her eyes. "If you tell us why, maybe we can help."

Noelia met the clear eyes of Sister Kelly. *What will they think of me? Do I dare tell them?*

"Please," said Sister Kelly, touching Noelia's shoulder. "You can trust us."

Noelia began to pick at her skirt. She'd never talked about this to anyone. Her eyes moved toward the darkness of the house but, of course, no one was there. No one could overhear. She looked back at the sisters. It would be such a relief to unburden her soul. Finally Noelia made her decision.

"I came to this house six months ago. My home is in Colombia. Santa Marta." Noelia paused trying to collect her thoughts. Perhaps she needed to explain Olivia first.

"When I was eighteen I meet a man, and I loved him. We are very close. When he knows I am pregnant, he goes away. I never see him again. Olivia, my daughter, was born."

Noelia didn't dare look at the sisters. She knew that it was wrong before God to be with a man who wasn't her husband. She stood up and began pacing the room as she continued her story.

"But Colombia is a very poor country. For a mother alone, is very hard to have child there. So I come to United States. My grandmother, she has a niece here, and she writes to her. She me *invitá*—she invite me to come live with her."

Noelia had been absently toying with a small piece of paper. When it slipped from her hand, she picked it up and stuck it in her pocket.

"In Santa Marta, I do good in my classes of English at school, so I go. My tia she buy the airplane ticket and take care of all the papers. I work, and I save money. Someday I bring Olivia to live in the United States with me. Is very hard to leave Olivia with my mother, but I know that is best . . . for our future."

She paused a moment. The missionaries were listening closely, and Sister Kelly gave her an encouraging smile. The next part was more difficult to explain.

"But I not know how mean is Tia Josefina. I come, and now I have no freedom. I am like *una esclava* . . . a slave."

Noelia leaned against the window, wondering how to make them understand how awful it had been.

"She is very bad lady. Does many things that are no honest. I cook and clean for her, and she pay me very little. She call me on telephone two times, maybe three times in a day, and if I not home . . . she is very, very mad." An involuntary shiver passed through her, and she glanced again at the empty doorway. Her fear of her tia was very real, and Noelia had no doubt that she was capable of doing almost anything.

"She is home always on Sunday. So you see why I can't have baptism?" Noelia returned to sit on the small wicker couch. "No is possible."

For a few moments, no one spoke, and then Sister Kelly broke the silence. "Do you really want to be baptized?" she asked.

"Yes, more than nothing," she said simply.

The sisters exchanged glances. Sister Prichert opened her quad and helped Noelia find the same verse in her Spanish scriptures. The older sister read aloud while Noelia followed along. "And it came to pass that I, Nephi, said unto my father: I will go and do the things which the Lord hath commanded, for I know that the Lord giveth no commandments unto the children of men, save he shall prepare a way for them that they may accomplish the thing which he commandeth them."

Sister Kelly tapped the cover of her scriptures. "We believe in miracles, and if you want this bad enough, then we are going to need to have enough faith. The Lord can make things possible even when we have no idea how to overcome a problem."

The same warm peaceful sensation that came when Noelia read the Book of Mormon flooded her heart now.

"Do you believe this?" asked Sister Kelly.

Noelia felt a deep assurance. "Si," she said.

"Okay, then," responded the sister missionary. "Let's do it."

They set a goal for Noelia to attend church the following Sunday. "It will take the prayers and faith of all three of us," Sister Kelly said. "But I know that Heavenly Father will find a way."

Noelia reached out and took each sister by the hand and squeezed. "Thank you."

Chapter Fifteen

ERICA SAT ON A DECK chair out in the backyard of Sister Shumway's home with a light shawl around her shoulders. The late October sun felt warm on her neck, and the soft wind ruffled her hair. She stared out at the yard around her, flipping absently through the Book of Mormon sitting open on her lap. It seemed as if she'd traveled to another planet rather than just a few miles from where she'd lived before.

The night before, when Sister Kelly and Sister Prichert had suggested she stay with an elderly lady in their ward, Erica had been dubious but too weak to protest. However, when she met the older woman, all Erica's doubts disappeared. Growing up, she'd never known a grandmother, but if she had, it would have been someone like Sister Shumway.

The guest room had a large bed, and the clean sheets smelled faintly of rose water as Erica slid between them. She'd fallen asleep as soon as her head hit the pillow and had awoken to the smell of frying bacon and freshly made waffles. Erica hadn't been pampered in a long time, and it made her feel a little self-conscious and unsure.

After the delicious breakfast, Sister Shumway had refused to let Erica help clean up, instead suggesting that the sunshine and fresh air in the backyard would do her a world of good.

Now, as she sat there, the breeze stirring the pages of the book in her lap, Erica felt as if she was in a scene from one of those old television shows like *Leave It to Beaver* or *Father Knows Best*. It was all so different from the way she'd lived her life, and Erica found herself wondering whether she could ever fit into this kind of an existence.

The back door opened and the older woman stepped outside. "Is there anything I can get for you?"

Sister Shumway was a petite woman well into her seventies. Her gray hair lay close to her head in tight curls, and vivid blue eyes peered out between the soft wrinkles on her face.

"No, I'm fine," Erica said, smiling back at her.

Sister Shumway untied a white apron from around her waist and tilted her face up toward the sun. "It's a nice afternoon," she observed. "You don't mind if I join you, do you, dear?"

"It's okay with me, Sister Shumway."

"Please, call me Emily. All my friends do." She turned back toward the house. "I'll just get my knitting."

Erica felt a warm sensation inside. It had been a long time since anyone had treated her with so much kindness.

Emily returned a few minutes later with a small wicker basket tucked under her arm and a gray knit sweater buttoned over her blouse. She drew up a chair next to Erica, sat down, and pulled out two knitting needles and about twelve inches of a brown and yellow afghan. For a few moments the two women sat companionably together, only the rhythmic sound of the knitting needles clicking together breaking the silence.

"This place is real nice," said Erica. "I like all the flowers and stuff."

Emily let her eyes wander around the yard. "Ed—my husband—loved to garden. You should have seen it when he was alive. Always perfect. I've hired a service to come mow the lawns each week, but it's not really the same."

"Don't your kids come over and help?" Erica asked.

"The good Lord didn't bless us with any children, I'm sorry to say." Emily sighed.

The sadness in the old woman's eyes made Erica feel uncomfortable, as if she'd accidentally touched an open wound. She sat there, unsure how to respond.

"I see you've got your Book of Mormon," Emily said, effectively changing the subject.

Erica rubbed a finger along the edge of the pages. "First thing anyone gave me I didn't have to pay for—one way or another."

"You haven't had an easy life, have you?" Emily asked.

"No," Erica said. "Being a prostitute is not an easy life."

She watched the older woman, waiting for some sign of disapproval or rejection, but instead the blue eyes were kind and understanding. Erica knew instinctively that she could trust this woman, even with her deepest feelings.

"I can't even imagine what you must have gone through," Emily said.

"You don't want to try. Out on the streets you gotta fight for every-thing—something to eat, fleabag bed to sleep on, the protection of the strongest pimp. I once saw a sixteen-year-old-get knifed over taking another girl's spot on the corner."

"I'm sorry," Emily murmured.

"Yeah, well, I'd probably still be there today if it hadn't been for the missionaries."

Emily had stopped her knitting and was leaning forward, listening with interest.

"One day I met these two guys in white shirts and ties standing at a booth in a mall. I needed some work and I thought, hey, maybe one of these Johns is looking for some lunchtime entertainment, you know? I hike up my mini to show a little more leg, and say, 'Hey baby,' like I've done a thousand times before. Only this time it was different."

Erica turned the closed book over and over in her hands.

"The first thing I noticed was the way they looked at me. They looked here"—she raised her finger up to her eyes—"not here," she said, pointing to her chest. "I never seen a guy do that before. To them we're just meat. Even the cops check out the goods when they bust us. But these guys—just boys really—looked me right in the eye like a real person. To be honest it freaked me out a little at first."

"I'll bet," Emily said as she finished off one row and began to knit back across.

"They said they weren't interested in my services and that they were missionaries," Erica continued. "I was so stupid, you know. I said it didn't matter to me."

"Then the taller one goes, 'No thank you,' real polite like. He looks right at me, takes this book from a pile on the table, and he says, 'Let me give you something instead.'"

Erica laughed at the memory. Back then, she'd had no idea what missionaries or the Book of Mormon were all about. All Erica knew was that these guys were different from anyone she'd ever met and maybe their book was too.

"Well, good for them," Emily said nodding her head in approval.

"And you know what he called me?" Erica asked. "He called me sister! You know, like I was someone."

Shifting to a more comfortable position on the chair, Erica continued. "I took the book home and read it, some of it anyway. I didn't understand a lot, but it made me feel good and clean."

Somewhere in the distance the sound of laughing children floated across the back fence.

"I hoped I'd run into them again. Tell 'em how I'd actually read the book. But they weren't at the mall the next time I went. And after a while I just kind of forgot about it. Then one afternoon I was watching TV and I saw this ad about Jesus. They were giving away a free Bible, and the guys on TV looked just like the two kids at the mall. I thought, why not? So I called the number and a few weeks later I met Sister Kelly."

Erica found herself laughing again as she remembered the look of shock on the young missionary's face when Sister Kelly realized what she did for a living. Erica set the book down in her lap. She'd known right away that the sister missionaries were unlike anyone she'd ever met. There was something about them that made her want to be better, maybe even change her life.

Looking around at the peaceful yard, Erica tried to imagine what it would be like to have a life like this. Nice house, maybe a husband and a couple of kids. But even as the idea formed itself in her mind, it seemed to drift away like smoke from the end of a cigarette.

"But now, I don't know . . ." She looked at the older sister. "I don't know where to go, what to do, or even who I am anymore."

Emily reached over and patted her hand. "You're a daughter of Heavenly Father, just like me."

Erica's laugh was short and hard. A parade of memories like slides flashing on a screen seemed to fill her head. "God don't want no daughter like me."

Emily tightened her grasp on the young woman's hand. "I don't think you understand. Heavenly Father is just like any parent who loves His children. No matter what, He's always there for us."

"Sure," Erica said, her voice bitter. "Just like my mom was there for me. No parent would want a kid that's done the things I've done."

The older woman's voice was gentle. "I don't know what happened between your mother and you, but I want you to know that if you were my daughter, I would be so proud of you."

Erica turned away. The emotional impact of the woman's words had been both strong and unexpected. She didn't know how to respond.

"Tomorrow is Sunday," Emily continued. "Why don't you come to church with me?"

"I don't know." Erica fidgeted with the end of her T-shirt. "I ain't never been in a church before. Always figured lightning would strike me if I did."

Emily raised her hand to her eyes and gazed up into the hazy blue sky. "The weather man says to expect sunshine all week, so you should be safe from electrical shock."

Erica smiled a little. "I'll think about it."

* * *

Tia Josefina looked up from the documents spread out on the desk in front of her and glared at her niece over the glasses balanced precariously on the end of her nose.

"*No es posible, mi hija,*" she said in Spanish then repeated herself in English. "It's not possible. I need you here on Sunday."

Noelia felt herself shrink back as her tia's attention returned to the papers before her. She'd put off asking for permission all week. Now it was Saturday night, and she couldn't put it off any longer. Taking a deep breath and trying hard to be brave, Noelia spoke again. "It wouldn't be for very long. Just an hour in the morning."

Tia Josefina slammed her hand down on the desk. "I said no. I have guests coming on Sunday and I will need you all day. Now leave! *Déjeme en paz.*"

"Si, tia," Noelia said hurrying out and rushing to her bedroom. The tears were flowing down her cheeks by the time she dropped to her knees by her bed. She buried her face in her arms and prayed softly, repeating over and over in Spanish, "Dear Father, I must go to your church to get baptized. Please provide a way."

It took a while, but slowly the fear drained away, and in its place Noelia felt enveloped by a warm sense of peace. She still had no idea how she was going to meet all the requirements for baptism, especially attending church, but it didn't seem to matter. Somehow it would work.

The next morning Noelia was up early making tortillas when her tia pushed open the kitchen door. "Don't worry about breakfast, *mi hija,* I'll grab a cup of coffee on my way out of town."

"You're leaving?" Noelia asked in surprise. "But what about your guests?"

"Change of plans. Raul just got a new boat and we're spending the day at sea. We may be back for an early dinner, though," she said over her shoulder. "I'll call around lunchtime and let you know."

Noelia watched the door shut softly and then smiled. She could hardly wait to call the sisters and tell them the good news, but first she knew that she needed to thank her Father in Heaven.

* * *

Amanda and her companion were waiting in the lobby when Noelia arrived at church. Sister Wilkie, a member who lived in the same neighborhood as their investigator, had stopped by and picked her up. The Colombian girl was dressed simply in a skirt and blouse, and her eyes were shining with excitement.

"I am happy to be here," she said, embracing the sisters and gazing around with interest.

Amanda watched her with delight. Everything about the sacrament meeting, from the organ prelude to the talks and prayers, was new and wonderful to Noelia.

I've attended hundreds of sacrament meetings in my life, Amanda thought looking around her at the familiar sights, *but today, seeing it all through Noelia's eyes, it makes me appreciate what a blessing it is.*

Noelia could only stay for the one meeting, and tears ran down her cheeks as she hugged the sisters good-bye.

"I love it here," she said. "The people, they are very good. Someday I can go to church every Sunday, and I will never miss a single day. Thank you for letting me come!"

Erica had also decided to attend church that Sunday, but for her the experience had clearly been much more difficult. She arrived with Sister Shumway, her Book of Mormon clutched to her chest. Erica was dressed in a tight belly shirt, short leather miniskirt, and tall black boots. Several people stared as she made her way down the aisle.

They slid into the pew next to the sister missionaries. Erica sat stiffly on the edge of her seat next to Amanda and spent much of the time looking around nervously and flipping the pages of her scriptures.

"Does it seem a little hot in here to you?" Erica asked, leaning over to Amanda during one of the talks. Her face was flushed, and a light layer of moisture made her forehead glisten.

"It's okay," Amanda assured her. "This is a good place for you to be."

Erica didn't look convinced.

Amanda watched her investigator out of the corner of her eye and silently prayed that Erica could feel welcome and accepted.

As the meetings progressed, Erica became more comfortable. Several people came up and shook her hand during Sunday School, and by Relief Society, Erica actually laughed with the other sisters at a funny comment the teacher made. Amanda was impressed by how friendly everyone in the ward was to her investigator.

The only exception was Sister Reynolds, a middle-aged sister with brown heavily teased hair who looked up as they walked into Relief Society and shook her head coldly. Amanda did her best to distract Erica, hoping she wouldn't notice the disapproving stare as they chose seats on the other side of the room.

Later that day, Sister Prichert told Amanda that the woman had pulled her aside after church.

"Perhaps you might want to prepare your investigators a little more before you bring them to church," the woman said, looking sternly over her cat-eye bifocals. "That girl looked like a tramp. I can imagine what the young men must have thought."

"What did you say?" Amanda asked.

"I just told her that the Lord invites all of His children into His house regardless of their appearance and I believe He expects us to do the same." Sister Prichert shook her head. "I think that some people are so busy being self-righteous they lose sight of the whole point. To love others as Christ loves us."

It was eight PM that Sunday evening, and the two sister missionaries were sitting in the living room of their apartment planning the next week.

"Other than that, I think things went pretty well today," Sister Prichert said. "Don't you?"

Amanda nodded, thinking back to the anxious feelings she'd had when Erica had first walked into the chapel. The young woman's leather miniskirt had looked exceptionally short when compared with the dresses of the other women in the meeting, and Amanda was sure that Erica had been wearing more makeup than usual, even for her.

"There must have been five sisters who went out of their way to welcome her," Amanda said. "I was so proud of them and grateful too."

"It doesn't surprise me, though," Sister Prichert said. "I really believe that some of the greatest women in the world are members of this Church!"

Her thoughts returned to Erica. Dressing modestly was one thing, but a complete transformation of lifestyle was something entirely different.

"Can you imagine Erica as a Primary teacher or an enrichment night leader?" Amanda asked her companion.

"It's certainly possible." Sister Prichert tapped the end of her pen against her chin. "But it would be a long, hard road, especially with her history. Plus, she doesn't seem to have the childlike faith that Noelia has. Still, I think it would be possible if she wanted it bad enough."

Amanda got up and headed to the kitchen for some string cheese and crackers. Her thoughts turned to the young Colombian girl. "I've no doubts about Noelia," she said, opening the refrigerator door. "I've never seen a person with as much desire as she has."

Sister Prichert followed Amanda into the kitchen. She poured herself a glass of water and shook out a blue pill from a plastic jar in her purse. "She made it to church today. That was the first hurdle."

Amanda sat down at the table with her food. "I can't get over how anxious she is to get baptized."

"That's true, but there's still a long way to go. Noelia must attend at least one more sacrament meeting and be interviewed by both the district leader and the mission president."

Although Sister Prichert didn't mention the additional challenge of getting Noelia out of the house long enough to be baptized, Amanda was aware that the words hung unspoken between them. *It will take a pretty major miracle.*

Suddenly a thought occurred to her. "The mission president?" Amanda asked, turning to her companion in surprise. "I thought she only had to meet with the DL."

"Usually that's true. But there are situations when the DL needs to refer someone on to the mission president as well—past chastity issues for example, and since Noelia has a baby out of wedlock . . ."

"Oh." Amanda leaned back in her chair. "So in other words, we are going to need to pray hard for Heavenly Father's help."

"Oh, yes," Sister Prichert agreed. "We're going to need all the faith we can muster."

* * *

Amanda was surprised and pleased to find that Sister Shumway and Erica had developed an immediate friendship. Emily invited Erica to live in her house for as long as she liked and had even started teaching the younger woman how to knit. Erica's bruises were healing, and she'd been out looking for a job.

The sisters had taught Erica many lessons, and she'd attended church for the last three weeks in a row, but despite her progress, Erica appeared more depressed each time the sisters visited. Amanda could sense her pulling away from them, but she didn't understand why.

After a prayer in the car, the sister missionaries knocked on Emily Shumway's door. It was three weeks until Thanksgiving, and Sister Shumway had decorated her entry with a large autumn wreath and a set of porcelain pilgrim figurines.

They'd decided that notwithstanding Erica's distant behavior, it was time to give her the baptismal challenge.

Sister Shumway answered and directed them into the living room where Erica sat flipping idly through a catalogue. She barely looked up when Amanda and her companion entered the room. They tried to draw her into conversation, but she refused to give more than a one- or two-word response.

Amanda looked over at her companion, who merely shrugged her shoulders in response to the unasked question. *What's going on? This isn't like Erica at all.*

"How is your reading of the Book of Mormon going?" Sister Prichert asked.

"I'm done," Erica said without looking up.

"That's great," Amanda said. "And did you pray about it?"

Erica closed the magazine but still wouldn't make eye contact. "Yeah, I prayed, and I know it's true."

Her voice held no pleasure, and the lack of reaction surprised Amanda. Sister Prichert frowned slightly.

This isn't the way it's supposed to go. Getting a witness of the gospel should bring joy and peace.

Amanda leaned forward slightly in her seat. "You got an answer to your prayer. You know it's true. That should be a good thing, right?"

For several moments Erica stared at her hands and didn't respond. When she finally looked up, there were tears in her eyes. "No, Sister Kelly, it isn't a good thing at all. Think about it." Erica gave a hard laugh. "Sure it's true, but so what? How's that gonna help me?"

"The same way it helps me," Amanda answered.

Erica shook her head and put her hands up to her face. "Sister Kelly, look at me. You know what I am. Okay, so all this church stuff works for you and Sister Prichert and Emily, but not for me. I've already blown my life. It ain't gonna happen. There's just no way."

Amanda felt an overwhelming rush of compassion and understanding for her investigator. At the same time, she had no idea what she could say that wouldn't sound trite or naive. For a few moments no one said a word. Then Sister Prichert broke the silence.

"Erica, do you remember when we talked about the Atonement last week? How Heavenly Father promised us that if a person will truly repent, they can be forgiven of their sins, no matter how bad they are?"

"Everyone can change," Amanda added but then found herself wondering. *Do I really believe that?*

"Everyone can change?" Erica said in amazement, "You're kidding, right? Can you see me as some pure little choir girl? It's too late. I made my choices and there are no second chances. I can't change what I am or what I've done. Take it away and there ain't nothing left."

Amanda poured out her heart in silent prayer. *Father, I need to know the answer. Can a person like Erica really change? Is it possible that someone can go from a life on street corners to a life of discipleship? Please, Father, tell me what to say.*

At first, Amanda felt nothing but the echo of her questions rising heavenward. Then the answer came. A tingly sensation spread from the top of her head all the way to her feet. With it came a peace that left no room for doubt. Amanda knew the answer. Now if she could help her investigator understand.

"Yes, I believe people can change," Amanda said with conviction. "You are God's child, and with His help you have the potential to be whatever you want to be."

"Maybe it works for somebody like you." Erica looked up, and Amanda could see the sheen of tears in her eyes. "But not for someone like me. God ain't gonna waste His time."

"Before you write yourself off, shouldn't you give Heavenly Father a chance?"

"For what?"

"To show you His love." The Spirit was in the room. Amanda sent up a silent plea that she would say the right words. "Pray. Ask God if He will forgive you, if you should be baptized. Give Him the opportunity to accept you."

Erica shook her head and turned away. "I can't."

"You've got to at least try," Amanda pleaded.

There was silence in the room for a long time. Amanda had to catch her breath when Erica finally turned back toward the sisters with eyes that reflected such great pain.

"Okay, I'll try. But don't expect no miracles from me. I'm a lost cause."

Not lost. Perhaps just a little misplaced.

Chapter Sixteen

AMANDA PULLED THE MISSION CAR up against the curb and parked it in front of Noelia's house. "I hate the feeling that we're sneaking around," Amanda said, reaching into the backseat to gather her books.

Sister Prichert nodded. "I know. Me too. But I keep reminding myself that this is an adult woman employed by a relative who is at best a bully and maybe even worse. She has every right to study the gospel if she chooses to."

Over the past few weeks, the sisters had continued to teach Noelia, but despite their best efforts and much prayer on her behalf, Noelia had been unable to leave her house to attend church.

Amanda had spent the last Sunday fasting on the young woman's behalf. It was clear to both of them that if the Lord didn't intervene, Noelia might never be baptized.

When the sisters arrived for their appointment, Noelia met them at the door, her eyes dancing with excitement.

"What is it?" asked Amanda. "Looks like you have some good news."

Her voice almost sang the words. "I am able to go to church this week!"

"Really? That's great." Amanda hugged her investigator. "But how did you manage it?"

"No me. Was God do it."

Noelia went on to tell them how the evening before, she'd prepared her tia's favorite dish, *Camarones a la Bogotá,* a shrimp dish with spices that would remind her of home. Noelia was hoping that her tia would enjoy the meal and that it would put her in a pleasant mood.

Tia Josefina arrived home on time and in excellent spirits. She had indeed enjoyed the dish and afterwards retired to her office to drink a glass of red wine and go over some papers.

It had taken every ounce of courage that Noelia could manage to walk into the room and ask if she could go to church the following Sunday.

"*Mi* tia—she think that I speak of the Catholic Church," Noelia said shyly. "And I no say nothing. She say that if I be home by ten-thirty to make breakfast I go."

"That's so wonderful." Amanda dropped down into one of the wicker chairs. In the sunroom the light on her shoulders felt as warm as the Spirit she felt inside her chest. "It seems like every time there's an obstacle, Heavenly Father makes a way to get around it."

Sister Prichert pulled out her planner. "We can probably schedule your baptismal interview on Sunday as well."

"Good idea," Amanda said.

"Sisters, there is something else." Noelia reached into the pocket of her dress, pulled out a small square of paper, and handed it to Amanda.

Turning the paper over, Amanda realized she was looking at a snapshot. It was well worn from much handling but still clear enough to recognize Noelia with a pretty, dark-haired child sitting happily on her lap.

"Is Olivia, *mi hijita*," Noelia said proudly. "My daughter."

Amanda studied the picture more closely. Olivia had her mother's eyes and smile, but the small cleft in the child's chin hadn't come from her mother. Amanda wondered about the father. Perhaps he would come back when he realized what a beautiful baby daughter he had, or maybe there was another who would love Noelia and her daughter. Amanda could almost imagine a gentle, dark-eyed man standing proudly beside his little family.

Family, Amanda thought in surprise. *Maybe this is the family I was meant to find?* She couldn't help the excitement that began to bubble up inside of her at the prospect.

"She's beautiful," Amanda said, her eyes moist as she handed the photo to Sister Prichert.

* * *

Sunday arrived and everything went as planned. Noelia was right on time for her baptismal interview with Elder Lopez. She came out fifteen minutes later with a huge smile on her face and sat with the sisters in the chapel listening to the soft prelude music from the organ.

Several people came over to greet her, including a good-looking young man who'd recently returned from a mission to Colombia.

"I fell in love with the whole country," he said to the sisters before shaking Noelia's hand. "*Tal vez podremos hablar después de los reuniones.*"

Noelia nodded back at him, too shy to respond, but it was evident that his attention had been welcome. Amanda thought again of the photo Noelia had shown her. She tried to readjust the picture in her mind, removing the dark-eyed man as the father and replacing it with the blue-eyed returned missionary they'd just met, but for some reason, he just didn't seem to fit.

After he left, Noelia leaned over and whispered in Amanda's ear, "Everyone is so kind. Someday I bring Olivia to church."

"I'm sure of it," Amanda agreed with confidence.

As it was the Sunday before Thanksgiving, all the talks and music were centered on gratitude. To Amanda it fit her own feelings perfectly.

After the meeting the sisters walked Noelia to the car. "All that's left is for you to meet with the mission president, and then you can be baptized," Amanda said.

"Can it be Monday or Tuesday?" Noelia asked. "Is very difficult to come at night or end of week. Tia Josefina is home."

"We'll call the president right away," Sister Prichert said, "and as soon as we have a time, we'll let you know."

Amanda hugged Noelia good-bye. "We're almost there."

"Si!" she agreed, looking happier than Amanda had ever seen her.

* * *

Noelia received the sisters' call late Monday afternoon. She picked it up on the first ring. Her tia arrived home earlier than expected with some business associates. They were having a meeting in the office and would then be served dinner. Usually the office phone was turned off during such occasions, but Noelia didn't want to take the chance that someone else might pick up the extension.

"Noelia," Sister Kelly said. "The mission president will meet you in his office at nine tomorrow morning. Sister Wilkie will be there at eight to pick you up. The drive should take forty minutes, so you'll be back before ten-thirty. No one will even know you were gone. It's perfect."

"Oh, thank you," Noelia said excitedly. "I will be ready, but I must get off now. Thank you so much, Sister! Good-bye!"

She hung up the phone and happily returned to the lettuce she was tearing for a salad. A moment later Tia Josefina stormed into the kitchen. Before Noelia realized what was coming, the other woman hit Noelia's face so hard that she fell against the wall and onto the floor. Before she could respond, Tia Josefina had grabbed a handful of her hair and was yanking her to her feet.

"You ungrateful *tramposa*," she screamed. "You abuse my hospitality by sneaking out of the house tomorrow to go to some man in the city, like a common prostitute."

"No," began Noelia, "that is not true. You don't understand."

"*Mentirosa*! Don't lie to me. I heard you on the phone. Did you think I wouldn't know what goes on in my own home?"

She released Noelia's hair and pushed her back against the wall. "You are a member of my household, and you obey me. If you ever leave this house again, for any reason, without my permission, you will be thrown out into the street. No one will help you and you will starve. You'll never see that daughter of yours again. Have I made myself clear?"

Noelia nodded. Her whole body was shaking and she felt ill.

"Now get this dinner served! My guests are hungry." She strode out of the room, slamming the door behind her.

For a few moments Noelia could do nothing but cry. Her face and left shoulder were bruised, but her tears were not for the physical pain. "Heavenly Father, what am I going to do?" she whispered.

She didn't dare call the sisters while her aunt was still in the house, so she spent a sleepless night in prayer and scripture study. Her feelings were torn. On the one hand, she was terrified of her tia, and she had no doubt that she would follow through on her threats. On the other, Noelia knew the gospel was true, and she couldn't rest until she had proven her faith to Heavenly Father by being baptized.

When the morning finally came, it was dark and gray. A storm seemed imminent, and Noelia nervously handed Tia Josefina her umbrella as she headed out to work. The older woman seemed preoccupied that morning, hardly saying a word as she left. As soon as the door closed behind her, Noelia turned toward the kitchen. She desperately needed to telephone the sisters to tell them what had happened and get their advice.

She'd only taken a few steps toward the phone when the door opened again and her tia returned.

"There's a FedEx package coming for me today," she said. "It will be here before ten o'clock. It needs to be signed for. I will call you later this morning to make sure it has arrived. It's a very important package."

Noelia swallowed hard, but Tia Josefina, assuming the girl's complete obedience, had already turned and was heading back outside.

* * *

The sister missionaries were just finishing breakfast when the call came through. In a few words Noelia explained about the scene with her tia the night before, the FedEx package expected that morning, and the call her tia had said she would make.

Amanda felt heartsick. The situation was getting dangerous, and, as much as she hated to suggest it, for Noelia's safety she thought it might be better to put off the interview for a few days or a week.

"No!" Noelia said firmly. "I must go. I must be baptized."

Amanda caught her breath at Noelia's insistence, wondering if she'd ever wanted something as badly as her investigator wanted this.

Staring out at the gray December sky, Amanda's fear for Noelia made her heart beat rapidly as she tried to think things through. *If she has the faith and the courage, do I have any right to stop her?*

"Sister?"

"I'm sorry. I was just thinking." Amanda pressed her index finger against her lips. "You're right. If we have enough faith, the Lord can make anything possible."

"I pray all night and I not scared. I believe if I trust, He will make everything okay."

Amanda closed her eyes hoping this was the right thing for Noelia to do. "We will pray, too."

After she hung up the phone Amanda turned to her companion. Sister Prichert had been listening, a worried look on her face, which became more pronounced as Amanda related Noelia's experiences.

Sister Prichert looked thoughtfully as she sat down on the couch. "I was afraid something like this might happen."

"You were?" asked Amanda. "Why?"

The older woman sighed. "Have you ever thought about how many people are affected when one man or woman chooses to be baptized?"

Amanda considered the question. "Well, there is the family of course, especially if there are children."

"That is true," she said, adjusting her glasses a little higher on her nose. "Having a parent or a spouse join the Church raises the chance that the rest of the family will join. But it's even larger than that. Think about all the extended family and friends who will be exposed to the Church as well."

Amanda leaned back against the table.

"Often the children will go on missions." Sister Prichert's eyes took on a glow of excitement. "And they spread the gospel to even more people."

Amanda could visualize a huge web of righteous influence, started by just one person joining the Church.

"And we haven't even mentioned the hundreds and thousands of ancestors on the other side waiting for ordinances that can only be completed by a temple worthy member."

Amanda stared at her companion in amazement. The prospect was overwhelming.

Sister Prichert continued. "So you see, one person's baptism can affect hundreds, maybe thousands of people. Is it any wonder that Satan works so hard against our converts, especially ones like Noelia that have such great faith?"

Again, the photo of Olivia, Noelia, and the father yet to be came into Amanda's mind. She could see why Satan would do anything in his power to stop their investigator from being baptized.

"I know you're right." Amanda dropped down on the couch beside her companion. "But understanding doesn't make it any easier to accept."

"No, it doesn't," Sister Prichert agreed, placing a hand on the young sister's arm. "All we can do is pray and trust Heavenly Father."

I feel so helpless, thought Amanda as a large truck rumbled down the street in front of the apartment complex causing the curtains in the front window to tremble. *There must be something we can do.*

She turned to Sister Prichert. "I won't be able to concentrate on anything today until Noelia gets back. Maybe we should drive over and wait at her house. We could sign for the FedEx package if she doesn't get back in time."

"I'm not sure they'd let us do that," Sister Prichert said. "And of course it won't help with the phone call, but I agree with you. Let's go over."

* * *

The rain had been falling steadily since Amanda and Sister Prichert had taken up their vigil across the street from Noelia's house. It made a rhythmic thrum on the roof of the car. The sisters alternated between prayers and watching the road for the first sight of Noelia's return. She'd been expected home by ten-thirty, and now it was after eleven. Fortunately the FedEx truck hadn't come yet either, but it could arrive at any moment, and Amanda felt sick with worry.

"What could have happened?" she asked for the third time that morning. "Do you think they got into an accident? The roads are really wet."

Sister Prichert shook her head. "I don't know."

Amanda stared at the rain streaming down the windshield as it broke off into dozens of little rivulets. She found her thoughts drifting back to a trip she'd made several years ago as one of four high school students chosen to represent the state at the prestigious Juilliard Music Competition. She remembered how certain she'd been of her chance to win first place in the French horn division.

Amanda and the other students had flown out of Salt Lake City and were scheduled to change planes in Minnesota before arriving in New York City late the night preceding the big event. However, an unexpected storm system moving across the central states had caused massive disruptions to the flights coming in and out of the St. Paul airport.

Amanda and her party were delayed five hours before the flight was cancelled altogether. Eventually they were given seats on a different airline and arrived at La Guardia three hours before the music competition was scheduled to begin.

It wasn't until all the other students had claimed their luggage and the baggage carousel had stopped moving that Amanda realized her French horn was missing.

She'd been frantic as she approached the airline representative's office. Without her French horn, she wouldn't be allowed to compete. In spite of her tearful pleadings, all they could suggest was to wait and see if the instrument turned up on a later flight.

One of the students had suggested they pray, asking Heavenly Father to bless them with a miracle. Amanda could still remember how hard she'd tried to overcome her fears and have faith that the horn would somehow appear in time.

However, in the end, it didn't arrive, and Amanda was forced to withdraw from the competition. A skinny little redheaded boy from Alabama had taken home the first-place award.

At the time, Amanda thought her world had come to an end, but looking back at it now, she realized how minor a setback it had been. Her French horn turned up a few days later, and she'd gone on to win many more competitions.

The fate that awaited Noelia if she didn't get back soon was much more serious. Even now, her tia might be trying to call, and if no one answered, the repercussions could be dangerous.

A brown Honda turned onto the street. "Look," shouted Amanda. "I think that's her!"

Sure enough the car pulled into the driveway of the green stucco house, and Noelia got out. Right behind them, a FedEx van pulled up, and a young man jumped out with a package under his arm.

The sister missionaries quickly crossed the street and were just in time to hear the deliveryman explaining his tardiness to Noelia.

"Gee, I'm so sorry this is late. The storm this morning caused some trouble with our planes landing, and then there was this major accident on the freeway that held up our distribution truck. You're the first delivery I've been able to make this morning."

Noelia signed her name and took the package. "No problem. I, too, just get home, so is good luck for me."

"I hope everyone else feels the same way," he said. "Though somehow I don't think they will. Have a nice day!"

"Thank you."

"Can you believe it?" asked Sister Wilkie. "We were stuck in traffic, and I thought for sure we wouldn't make it home in time, but it turns out the gridlock was on our side."

The sound of the phone ringing from within the house caught everyone's attention, and Noelia unlocked the door and rushed in to answer it.

She came back out a few minutes later, her eyes wide in amazement.

"My tia, she say that the phones down all morning and her cell phone no go through until now."

Amanda turned toward Sister Prichert in amazement. Her companion could only shake her head.

Wow, I am never going to forget this moment or the power of Heavenly Father to those who have faith in Him.

Chapter Seventeen

ERICA KNELT BY THE SIDE of her bed. A soft breeze blew through the window and swept her hair. She'd been putting this off for nearly a week, but she'd promised Sister Kelly that she'd pray. Despite all her faults, Erica was a person of her word.

She thought about the things that the sister missionaries had taught her—how she lived with Heavenly Father before she was born. Erica wondered what type of a person she was back then, before life happened to her.

Her thoughts passed on to her mother. The few childhood memories Erica had were disjointed and incomplete. She couldn't remember the woman's face, but for some reason the smell of lilacs had always made Erica think of her. Her mother was dead now. Erica felt certain of that, but the idea that she might be out there somewhere in the cosmos watching filled Erica with a sense of both comfort and dread.

She tried to focus on the task at hand, closing her eyes and pressing her forehead against the soft surface of the quilt.

"Father," she began. "I've done a lot of things that are wrong."

Boy, that's an understatement, she thought as memories from the past flew unbidden into her mind, filling her soul with a deep darkness. It was torturous, and for a few moments, Erica could have sworn that she remembered each individual sin she'd ever committed.

Tears filled her eyes as the enormity of what she'd done overwhelmed her. How could God ever forgive all that?

"Father," she called again. This time it was not a question, but a desperate cry for help—a pleading for divine relief. "Oh, Father!"

Erica waited—feeling abandoned, the anguish washing over her again and again. She was wracked by guilt and surrounded by a sense of despair so tangible she thought it might destroy her. "Oh, Father!"

How long she remained in that desperate state, Erica wasn't sure, but little by little, she became aware that the pain was subsiding, and in its place, a warm sense of peace and love filled her. It grew stronger until she felt that her whole being must be radiating.

Tears still ran down her cheeks, but they were no longer tears of suffering. Instead they were tears of joy. A voice came to her—whether from within or without she was never quite sure. It was audible nonetheless and ran through her body like a current of electricity. "Go and sin no more. You will be forgiven."

Erica knelt there in the dark, her face in her hands, enveloped by that incredible sensation. She couldn't explain what had happened to her; she didn't really want to try. But one thing Erica did know for certain: she would never be the same again.

* * *

Amanda awoke before the alarm went off. In a few hours Noelia would be baptized. What a wonderful way to end her mission!

She smiled to herself as she imagined the young girl dressed in white, walking down the stairs of the baptismal font where Elder Lopez would be waiting to perform the ordinance.

And afterwards, what? The question came unbidden into her mind, and Amanda considered it for a moment. She'd been so caught up in simply getting Noelia baptized she hadn't given much thought to what would happen next.

She'll probably end up moving in with a member family. The ward employment specialist could help her find a job, and there's that young man from church who served his mission in Colombia.

Amanda sat up in bed and swung her legs down, pushing her feet into the fluffy blue slippers she'd kicked off the night before.

Of course, there's also the possibility that she'll want to go home to her daughter. Amanda stood and looked around for her robe. *Either way, I carried out my assignment. When Noelia and Olivia go to the temple, they will be together for eternity.*

In a way it was a relief to finally have her dream confirmed after giving up so much. Her family had received an invitation to Jake's wedding, and her mother had written, "Jake's wife is kind of young and not nearly as pretty as you are, but she's here."

And I'm not.

For a while Amanda had felt resentful and angry with Jake. She'd waited for him for two whole years while he was on his mission, but he hadn't even been able to make it through one. It had been painful for a while, but thankfully, she was over the worst.

Now, as Amanda opened the blinds, the sun streamed through the bedroom window, and she felt a sense of acceptance. *Being able to see this wonderful day happen is worth everything I had to give up.*

The sisters arrived at the church early to make sure that the font had been filled and the chairs set up. A small, artificial Christmas tree stood in the foyer decorated with ornaments the Primary children had made. Christmas was only three weeks away, and Amanda would be going home on Christmas Eve. This might well be her last baptism in the field.

They weren't expecting many people on a Tuesday morning, but there would be enough to complete the ordinance. The bishop had taken off work to preside. The mission president and his wife had also decided to attend.

It was nearly time to start when Sister Wilkie arrived. "I went by the house to pick up Noelia and no one was home," she said, trying to catch her breath. "I knocked and knocked. I think the place is empty!"

"That's not possible," Amanda said. "I talked to her two days ago. She's got to be there." Amanda frowned at her companion. "You don't suppose something happened to her, do you?"

"I don't know, but if her tia somehow found out about the baptism . . ." Sister Prichert didn't complete the thought. She didn't have to.

"Sister Wilkie, will you explain to the bishop what's happening?" Amanda was already fishing in her purse for the car keys. "Tell him we're going to Noelia's house and that we'll be back as quickly as possible."

"Okay," the other woman responded, but the two sister missionaries had already rushed out the door.

Amanda drove as quickly as she could, a myriad of frightening possibilities racing through her head.

Something must have happened. She never would have missed this day unless . . .

The house came into sight, and a large moving truck was parked backward in the driveway. Several men in gray jumpsuits were going in and out of the front door carrying boxes and pieces of furniture.

Amanda rushed up and grabbed the arm of a passing worker. "Excuse me," she said. "But do you know where the people are who own this house?"

"No hablo inglés," said the man, shaking her off of his arm and returning to his work.

"Well, does anyone around here *hablo inglés?*" Amanda cried in frustration.

Sister Prichert came up beside her. "Let's try to find the person in charge. He'll probably speak English."

They entered the house and looked around. Some of the furniture had already been removed, and other pieces were still waiting to be taken.

"Maybe she's upstairs." Amanda turned and ran up the staircase.

The rooms above were already empty, devoid of any character or personality.

"I don't understand. How can someone just up and move without any warning?"

Sister Prichert put an arm around her young companion. "I'm sure she's okay. Come on, there's bound to be someone around that knows what happened."

Downstairs they were able to locate a mover who spoke English.

"I don't know where they went." He consulted a clipboard. "I was told to pack everything into storage. That's all I know."

"But this makes no sense," Amanda said. "We were here last week, and no one said anything about moving."

"*Con cuidado,* Antonio!" the man yelled in Spanish before turning back to Amanda. "Look, lady, all I know is we got the order Monday. As you can see, the place is vacant. I'm sorry, but I've got a lot of work to do."

Sister Prichert led Amanda out of the house and back to the car. "There's nothing more we can do, Sister Kelly. We'll just have to wait and hope Noelia contacts us."

"But this isn't right! She's supposed to be baptized today. After all the other things the Lord has done to make this possible, how can she just disappear?"

"I'll bet she calls tonight or tomorrow," Sister Prichert said. "She wanted this very badly. She isn't going to just walk away from it now."

"I hope you're right."

But Noelia didn't call that night or the next. Days went by without word from her. Then an entire week. Finally, Amanda had to accept it—Noelia wasn't coming back.

* * *

The next week went by in an emotional blur. Amanda's parents called to verify her flight information. It was good to hear her mother's voice on the other end of the phone. Images of home came rushing into her mind. She found herself eager to be with her family again.

Yet, at the same time, Amanda felt depressed.

For days she'd grieved the loss of her investigator. Amanda had been so sure that Noelia and her daughter were the people from her dream. But evidently she'd been wrong, and now her mission was drawing to a close and time was running out.

The news that Erica had received an incredible spiritual witness cheered Amanda immensely. She listened in amazement as the young woman recounted the experience.

"If you'd said a month ago that God would talk to someone like me, I would have said you were a liar." Erica looked down at the floor. "But as strange as it seems, He did talk to me, and now I know that He loves me."

The emotion in Erica's voice set off a strong echoing response within Amanda's own breast.

She stared at her friend in amazement. *I've never seen her like this.*

The transition was difficult to describe, but there was indeed something different about Erica. She appeared to stand a little straighter with a light and happiness about her countenance that hadn't been there before.

"I guess I was wrong," Erica said, grinning at Amanda. "There are second chances in life. Even for people like me."

Amanda could only nod. She didn't trust her voice. She thought about how she'd been blessed to witness so many miracles in the past eighteen months—more than her share. She'd grown more than she would ever have thought possible.

Amanda recalled the night in the MTC so many months before, when she'd poured out to her companion the great fear she had of making mistakes during her mission. *There's no doubt that I've messed up many times. But with Heavenly Father's help, it's been okay, and I've learned so much.*

Yet, despite the joy she felt for Erica, Amanda couldn't shake the nagging guilt that she'd been unable to complete her special commission. Sure, she'd taught many people, some of who had chosen to join the Church, but Amanda was certain that she hadn't found the family from her dream.

"What do I need to do now?" Erica asked, her eyes bright and excited.

"You'll need to talk with President Edwards." Sister Prichert checked her planner. "Perhaps this Saturday will work."

"Just tell me when the interview is, and I'll be there."

Amanda smiled as she watched her investigator.

Maybe it didn't matter. Maybe the fact that I tried was enough. One thing Amanda did know for certain: whether she found her family or not, it was moments like this when she knew for sure that coming on a mission had been worth the sacrifice.

A few days later, Amanda and Sister Prichert were sitting in the lobby of their ward building waiting for Erica to come out of her interview with the mission president.

"How long do you think she'll be?" asked Amanda, looking at her watch for the sixth time since Erica had gone in. "It's been an hour already."

"It will take as long as it takes," Sister Prichert said, glancing up from the *Ensign* article she was reading.

"Erica was so nervous before she went in. I hope everything goes okay."

"President Edwards is a good man," Sister Prichert said. "I'm sure he has the Spirit with him."

"That's true," Amanda said, staring at the office door in front of them.

In the last few days, Erica had been a transformed woman. The depression had left, and in its place was a carefree gladness.

Amanda stood up and looked out through the glass doors. "It's just so amazing. Who would have believed that someone could change so much in such a short period of time?"

"That's for certain," Sister Prichert said. "This will definitely be a story for my journal."

A few minutes later the office door swung open as President Edwards and Erica stepped out.

"You are a unique young lady," President Edwards said as he took her hand in his. "I admit, I don't know if I would have the strength to do what you are about to do."

Erica looked around, clearly uncomfortable. "Uh, thanks, President."

"Good luck, and may the Lord bless you," he said.

As Sister Prichert hugged Erica, Amanda pulled President Edwards aside. "I wanted to ask if there was any way I could possibly extend my mission," she said. "I just feel like it's too soon to go home. And I know my family would understand."

President Edward smiled warmly. "Sister Kelly, I would love nothing better than to have you stay, but the Lord needs you home now."

"I thought that was what you would say," Amanda said with a shrug, "but I had to at least suggest it."

"So," Amanda asked as soon as they'd left the building, "how did it go? What did you say? What did he say?"

"Sister Kelly," chided her companion. "They were having a private meeting."

"It's okay," Erica said, chuckling. "There's nothing you two don't know about me. I told him everything."

She was quiet for a moment, a faraway look in her eye. "It was hard. Ugly and dirty, you know? I thought he would be disgusted, but he just looked at me all nice and everything. He says how Heavenly Father loves me. That it's possible to be forgiven. I can be clean, he says."

Amanda's heart was overflowing with love, and she reached out and hugged the young woman.

Erica hugged her back. "Hey, there's more. He says if everything is okay and I do stuff right, I can be baptized in six months."

Amanda understood fully. With the lifestyle that Erica had been living, the leaders were bound to be cautious.

"Don't worry. I'll fly back for your baptism. Nothing could keep me away," Amanda said.

Erica blew her nose. "Actually, I had another idea."

* * *

The San Jose airport lobby was busy as usual. Before passing through security, the seven missionaries who were leaving that day visited with each other and friends they had made during their mission who had come to see them off.

Amanda stood a little to one side. In some ways it seemed like she'd arrived yesterday, but in others it was as if a whole lifetime had passed. She wasn't the same girl she'd been eighteen months ago.

Sister Baker, Amanda's MTC companion, came up and hugged her. "So you made it. I knew you would."

"Looks like we both did." Amanda looked at her old friend. Sister Baker had lost a few pounds, and her hair was a little shorter, but other than that, the girl hadn't changed much. "I bet your family can't wait to see you!"

"Yeah. It sounds like they're gonna have a family reunion right there in the airport lobby."

Sister Baker drifted off to speak with another missionary, and President Edwards took her place. He reached out to shake Amanda's hand. "We're really going to miss you around here."

"Thanks, President. You're sure I can't talk you into letting me stay a little longer?"

"I don't think your folks would be too thrilled if I did that," he said, laughing. "Besides, I understand you're taking a souvenir home with you. Is that right?"

Amanda motioned toward the gift shop where Erica stood looking through the magazine racks.

"Thank you for helping her to go back with me," Amanda said.

"I thought her chances for a new life were better in Provo than out here. You won't have any trouble finding her a place to stay, will you?"

Amanda smiled. "It's all taken care of. She's got a little money saved, and my parents have offered to pitch in too. We're going to share an apartment, and she wants to get into beauty college."

"Let me know who your new bishop is and I'll give him a call. I'm sure he'll be anxious to help Erica make it to her baptism."

"I will," promised Amanda.

"How about you?" President Edwards asked. "What are your plans for the future?"

"Graduate school," Amanda said without hesitation. "I was accepted before I left, and BYU is good about working with returned missionaries."

"I would imagine."

Erica paid for her purchases and came up to join Amanda and the mission president.

"Thanks for everything," Erica said. "Sure you can't come in June for my baptism?"

"I wish I could," he said. "Why don't you send me some pictures? I would sure love to see you all dressed in white!"

"That'll be something," agreed Erica.

Amanda looked down at her watch. "Our flight leaves soon, and we still need to pass through security."

President Edwards reached into his jacket pocket. "This came in today's mail. The APs managed to pick it out and give it to me before I left."

Amanda took the blue aerogram, noting the Colombian return address.

"Send me an e-mail after you get home and let me know how she's doing," he said, tapping the letter in her hand.

Amanda assured him that she would and said her good-byes before stuffing the envelope into her pocket and heading to security. Erica was right behind her, a couple of magazines sticking out of her massive purse.

They hurried down the long airport corridor only to discover that the incoming flight had been delayed because of bad weather in Chicago.

"Are the planes often late?" Erica asked. "It's not any kind of mechanical failure, is it?"

"These flights are never on time," Amanda said, sitting down on a hard plastic chair.

Erica sat next to her and popped a stick of gum into her mouth. "I was thinking of calling some old friends to say good-bye." She looked toward a bay of pay phones against the wall.

"I think it's a good idea. We've probably got another hour's wait at least."

"I'll be back," Erica said, rising from her chair and digging in her purse until she found some change.

Amanda waited until the young woman was gone before pulling the aerogram out of her pocket and unfolding it on her lap. It was written in small, careful print—Noelia's handwriting.

Dear Sister,

I so sorry that I leave and no say good-bye. My tia became in trouble and we had to leave suddenly at night. I wished to telephone but there no was time. Please forgive me. I back home now with Olivia. She is so big. Is good at home and I am happy.

I find sister missionaries here and they take me to church. I was baptized last week. My mother and my little brother was baptized, too. Next year I go to temple. Perhaps you come?

I am thankful for you and for Sister Prichert and for gospel of Jesus. I go to church every Sunday. Thank you so much, Sister!

Con Carino,
Noelia Mora

Amanda set the letter down and stared through the huge glass window at an airplane waiting across the tarmac. The realization that Noelia was safe and that both she and several members of her family had been baptized left Amanda with a sense of peace, but she also felt disconcerted.

Noelia must have been the one from my dream after all. It didn't happen the way I'd imagined, and I didn't get to witness the baptism myself, but I always felt like she was part of the family from my dream.

During the past eighteen months, Amanda had often fantasized how it would be when she finally found the family she'd been searching for. But now that it had happened, Amanda felt let down. Perhaps, over time, she'd built the whole thing up in her mind so that the fantasy became more powerful than the reality.

She sighed. It didn't matter though. Noelia was baptized, and Amanda could go home knowing that she'd done what she had been sent to do.

"Miss Amanda Kelly, please pick up a courtesy phone. Miss Amanda Kelly, please pick up a courtesy phone."

The disembodied female voice floated over the loudspeaker, and Amanda looked up. She was almost certain she'd heard her name called, but who could be paging her? Perhaps she'd left something at the mission office, or maybe there was an emergency at home. Amanda got up quickly.

"I'm Sister Kelly," she said into the courtesy phone.

"Yes, Miss Kelly. You have a party waiting for you at the Delta information desk in the lobby."

"Are you sure?" Amanda asked. "Do you know who it is?"

"I'm sorry, I don't, ma'am. I just know that someone requested to have you paged."

"Thank you," Amanda said automatically as she hung up and headed back up the long corridor. She wracked her brain, trying to think of a reason that someone might need to reach her before the flight left, but it remained a mystery. *I hope there's nothing wrong.*

She passed the security station and entered the ticketing area. Several yards away a dark-haired woman stood looking in Amanda's direction and waving frantically. "Sister Kelly, Sister Kelly!"

Amanda stopped in confusion. The woman looked vaguely familiar, and for some reason her stomach sank uncomfortably.

"Sister Kelly, over here," the woman called again and began running toward her.

Suddenly the memory flooded back. This was the woman Amanda had sat next to on the plane ride from Salt Lake to San Jose, seventeen months earlier.

"I'm sure you don't remember me," the woman said, stopping a few feet from Amanda. "But I met you on a flight out of Utah over a year ago. My name is Lyn, Lyn Frazier."

"I remember," Amanda said. The sight of Lyn and the memory of their conversation on the plane brought back all the feelings of frustration and discouragement she'd felt that day so many months before. *I can't believe she remembers my name or that she'd take the trouble to find me.*

"I couldn't let my missionary leave without saying good-bye now, could I?"

"*Your* missionary?" Amanda stared at her. The woman made as much sense as if she was speaking Swahili. "I don't understand."

"I know you don't, but that's okay. I just needed to apologize," Lyn said. "I was awful to you before. I was so bitter and angry, and there you were trying to share your testimony with me. I'm so sorry!"

Amanda shook her head in bewilderment. Everything seemed surreal—as if this were a dream. *Did the woman come all this way just to apologize for being short with me?*

"If it's any consolation, after I left that day, I couldn't get you off of my mind," Lyn continued. "The things you'd said made me feel something I didn't want to feel. I tried to forget about it, get back to my life, but I couldn't help myself. Sometimes I would wake up at night and your words would haunt me. Finally I broke down and called the phone number on that pass-along card. These two young elders came out and taught me. Then two more came out and two more after that."

Lyn looked down at her shoes and blushed. "It took me a whole year before I was able to accept Heavenly Father and be baptized. But last August I did it."

Amanda couldn't believe what she was hearing. Could it be true? Had Lyn really felt the spirit of her testimony after all?

"Ever since then, I've wanted to find you and thank you, but for some reason I thought you were in the San Francisco mission. The president of the mission there has been trying to track you down for months. This morning he called and said that he'd found you here in San Jose but that you were leaving today. He even managed to get your flight schedule. I rushed as fast as I could, but I was afraid I'd missed you."

"The flight was delayed."

"I guess Heavenly Father was helping me out again," Lyn said as she took a step forward and put her arms around Amanda's shoulders and hugged her tightly. Amanda hugged her back, brushing the woman's dark hair with her cheek and smelling the faint scent of lilac perfume.

"I just had to come and find you," Lyn said, stepping back. "I knew I needed to talk to you before you left. I had no choice!"

"I'm so glad you did. Thank you for letting me know."

"At last! I got off the phone and you'd disappeared." Amanda turned at the sound of Erica's voice and found the young woman standing behind her. In all the excitement, she'd completely forgotten her friend.

"I'm sorry, I should have told you I was leaving. Lyn, this is a good friend of mine, Erica. She's going back home with me."

"Your name is Erica?" Lyn said, a strange note in her voice.

"Yeah," Erica responded. "Why?"

"No reason." Lyn studied the girl's face closely, as if she looked familiar. "I always liked that name. Do you know anyone with the last name Smith?"

Erica nodded. "That's my last name. Why?"

The strange look on the older woman's face puzzled Amanda. Was it possible that Lyn knew that Erica had once been a prostitute? The idea seemed far-fetched, and yet Amanda could think of no other reason to explain the older woman's intense scrutiny.

"Why are you looking at me like that?" Erica asked, taking a step back. She shot a nervous glance at Amanda.

Lyn didn't respond. She just kept staring.

"What's going on?" Amanda turned to Lyn, but the older woman didn't answer. She continued to gaze at Erica with a strange light in her eyes.

"This is too weird," Erica said, reaching out to Amanda. "Let's get out of here."

"I had a little girl named Erica once," Lyn said slowly, never taking her eyes from Erica's face. "She was taken from me when she was five."

What is she saying? Amanda caught her breath.

Erica's face was pale and her eyes huge, but she didn't move away.

"My little girl was born April 18," continued Lyn. "She'd be twenty-four this year, and my maiden name, the last name of my daughter, was Smith."

Erica swallowed. "I'm twenty-four," she said, "but there must be thousands of other girls . . ."

"She had beautiful dark hair just like yours, and she liked to watch me put on my makeup. I'd always dab my lilac perfume on her wrists."

"Lilac," Erica whispered.

Amanda turned from one woman to the other. The air was charged with a tension that she didn't understand.

"It isn't possible," Erica said.

Lyn didn't respond. She just kept staring.

"Mom?" The question choked out of Erica and seemed to hang in the air between them.

No one moved. Amanda held her breath. Then Lyn raised her hand to her lips, her eyes bright with unshed tears. She took a few hesitant steps toward Erica then reached out the same hand and gently touched her daughter's cheek. "I've found you," she whispered. "I've found you at last."

Erica didn't move at first, but then slowly she raised her own hand until it covered the one that rested on her cheek.

Amanda's heart began to beat faster as she watched the drama taking place in front of her. It was as if the world had been shaken apart and now the pieces were falling back into place.

Erica spoke first. "When you didn't come back I figured you were dead."

"Oh, sweetheart." Lyn's brow creased in lines of sorrow. "I tried. I was sick, and then when I got well, I couldn't find you. I never wanted to lose you. You've got to believe that!" Her voice shook, and in an instant they were embracing. Amanda looked away, trying to hold her own tears back.

"You found my baby," Lyn said to Amanda over the young woman's shoulder. "But how?"

As her eyes rested on the mother and daughter reunited after so many years, Amanda had a sudden rush of understanding. It wasn't Noelia after all. This was the family she'd been sent to find, to put back together. As the realization hit her, she felt an overwhelming sense of humility, joy, and gratitude to Heavenly Father for allowing her to share this moment with them. She responded in the only way she could think of. "She wasn't lost to Heavenly Father."

Epilogue

Nine Months Later

AMANDA ALWAYS LOVED THE START of autumn in Utah—the changing colors of the leaves, the brisk chill in the air, and the start of a new school year. Walking across the BYU campus, she watched the freshmen scurrying between classes looking lost, while the upperclassmen and graduate students like herself were happily greeting professors and classmates.

But this fall would be her last at the university. In December, Amanda was expecting to graduate with her master's degree in English literature. The fact that she would soon be leaving BYU gave everything around her a bittersweet feeling.

Amanda was considering an internship with a New York magazine after graduation, but nothing was set. All she knew for sure was that in a few months, a part of her life she'd grown to love would be over forever. It was sad but a little exciting at the same time.

She hurried toward the Cougareat where Erica and Lyn Frazier were meeting her for an early lunch.

"I'm not late, am I?" Amanda asked, throwing her books down in an empty chair.

Lyn laughed. "You're right on time. We only got here a few minutes ago. What do you think of Erica's new style?" She pointed to her daughter across the table and giggled. The girl's normally dark hair was now a vivid shade of plum.

"It's the new red," Erica said as if that would explain it all.

Erica had been in beauty school for six months and was hoping that with her mother's financial help and expertise in the field, she could open her own salon downtown once she graduated.

"Well, it certainly matches your outfit," Amanda said, trying to keep a straight face.

"Don't worry," Lyn confided. "You know she never keeps a style for longer than a month."

"I'm thinking about colored contacts," Erica said. "Maybe tiger eyes or something."

"That would be attractive," said Amanda with just a little sarcasm.

Erica had adjusted well to Latter-day Saint life. She was active in her singles ward, even teaching Relief Society, but she had shied away from the dating scene. And she was seeing a therapist to cope with the scars from her past.

"That's my girl," Lyn said, winking at Amanda. "Always on the cutting edge of fashion."

Lyn had made three trips out to Utah to get reacquainted with her daughter. It was a little rocky at first, dealing with the pain of the past. However, with time, the two had developed a close relationship.

Three months ago, Lyn had sold her beauty franchises in the bay area and moved out to Utah. She'd found a job as a manager for one of the larger cosmetology schools and bought a condo in Provo.

The two had even taken a trip down to Arizona to meet Erica's birth father. Will was a widower of five years and, according to Erica, there still appeared to be an attraction between Lyn and him. Will asked a lot of questions about their new religion, and plans were in the works for him to come up to Utah for Thanksgiving.

"We have a surprise for you," Lyn said, pulling a large parcel wrapped in brown paper out of her enormous shoulder bag.

"Another hair-care product you want me to try?" Amanda eyed the package with curiosity.

"No, not this time." Lyn slid it across the table. "Erica and I had some pictures taken together a while ago. One of them came out pretty good, and we thought you might like a copy."

"Of course I would," Amanda said as she began tearing off the wrap. "I can't wait to see it."

She peeled off the paper and then caught her breath as she removed the contents: a shiny ornate gold frame surrounded an eight-by-ten portrait of a happy looking Lyn and Erica. Amanda felt the hairs on the back of her neck rise. She recognized the frame immediately. It was the same one she'd seen hanging on the wall in her dream.

"Are you okay?" Lyn asked, a look of concern on her face.

For a moment Amanda couldn't speak. Tears filled her eyes and she smiled at them both.

"It's wonderful," Amanda said, laughing a little to get past her emotions. She'd never told either one of them about her dream, so they had no way of knowing how the picture had led her to serve a mission. It could only be another miracle.

About the Author

DEANNE BLACKHURST WAS BORN IN Oakland, California. She's lived in many places across the United States and served a year-and-a-half mission in the Paraguay Asuncion Mission. Deanne spent over ten years researching the experiences of sister missionaries throughout the world and conducted in-depth interviews with over thirty-five young and older sisters who served as single sister missionaries in places as common as Idaho or as far-flung as Russia.

She has six children, a son-in-law, a darling grandson, and she lives with her husband, Kent, in Pleasant Grove, Utah.